Molly Justice

A story of Molly Maguires and Modocs in the
Mahanoy Valley of Pennsylvania.

by Steve Varonka
Illustrations by Leslie Young

10/6/01
Carrie + George
Enjoy my Molly tale.
Peace + long life

Coal Hole Productions

Bloomsburg, PA 17815

www.coalhole.com

Cover art and illustrations by Leslie Young

This book is a work of fiction. Names, characters, places, and incidents either are products of the author's imagination or are used fictitiously. Any resemblance to actual events or locales or persons, living or dead, is entirely coincidental.

ISBN 0-9709630-0-9

Published by:
Coal Hole Productions
Bloomsburg, PA 17815
www.coalhole.com

Acknowledgments

Writing a book can be a stressful, painful process if those around you are not supportive. I have been extremely lucky to receive a great deal of support and understanding. For this reason I thank my wife Joan for not thinking this to be just another Ralph Cramden venture.

I also want to thank Mary Jane Memolo and George Turner for their first reading and critical commentary.

Lastly, I want to thank Eric McKeever and Christine Goldbeck for establishing the Coal Region Book Nook to support regional authors and MineCountry.com which keeps interest in coal region history alive.

Dedication

This work is dedicated to my Casserly ancestors

1	Bernard Casserly	1820 -
	+Catharine	1830 -
2	Bridget Casserly	1855 -
2	Catherine Casserly	1859 -
2	Patrick Casserly	1852 - 1918
	+Catherine Leonard	1852 - 1900
3	Elizabeth K. Casserly	1878 - 1928
3	Katherine C. Casserly	1880 -
3	Michael Casserly	1881 - 1918
3	Bernard M. Casserly	1877 - 1934
	+Sarah M. Dreisbach	1880 - 1938
4	Bernard Casserly	- 1956
4	Anna Casserly	1906 -
4	John James Casserly	1916 -
4	Patrick J. Casserly	1899 - 1966
	+Miriam C. Albright	1901 - 1987
5	James Patrick Casserly	1921 - 1986
5	Bernard Casserly	1923 - 1992
5	Joseph Casserly	
5	Marion Isabel Casserly	1919 - 1996
	+Walter Varonka	1923 - 1954

Introduction

When I was back in Mahanoy Area High School if you had told me that one day I would write a story about Mahanoy City, much less a historical-based one, I would have told you that you were insane. If there was one thing I hated more than English it was History. Well here it is, a story about 1875 Mahanoy City. It was a tumultuous time, the height of the Molly Maguires. Coal mining was a growing industry, one that would fuel the industrial revolution. We could not have an industrial revolution without some growing pain. This pain was endured by the Irish immigrant and later by the eastern European immigrants. Cultural prejudice and class distinction were the norms. The Irish had left a country with a 700-year history of cultural and class prejudice. Many had left to flee starvation, others followed to build a new life, a free life.

So what inspired me? The answer is, my roots. I, like many others, felt the need to find out where I came from. Who were my ancestors? I thought it would not take very long since my father's parents had immigrated only in the 1890's. They came from the Carpathian-Rusyn area known as Galicia, today in southern Poland. They were Rusyn's, not to be confused with Russians. My mother's parents, Irish, can't go back more than the 1850's famine immigration. That was true. Ah, but the Pennsylvania Germans would show up as well. Turns out I have two Civil War veterans and one War of Independence veteran who also signed the Pennsylvania constitution. What a journey it has been.

So why a Molly Maguire book? As I did my research, I kept running into the Mollies. I also found interest in a Sunday morning radio show called "The Orange and the Green Show." It is run each week by two colorful Irishmen who will not let you forget your Irish roots. So I decided to learn more and began to read. I was hooked. I started to wonder if my ancestors were Mollies. Well there was really no way to find out. I started to think what it might have been like for the Irish that were not members of the Ancient Order of Hibernians. The population of Mahanoy City in 1875 was probably around 6500 with a high percentage of Irish. According to a list leaked by the Pinkerton Detective Agency there were only 21 A. O. H. members in Mahanoy City. An odd ratio I thought and that started the book idea.

The book follows a historical time line that I pieced together from my reading. The story is entirely fictional. I intentionally leave the historical references vague to keep the plot flowing. I did not want to write another Molly history. I'll leave that to the historians.

If you are knowledgeable of the period, you will immediately pick up on the references. My hope is that you can enjoy the book with little historical knowledge and might be prompted to research the history on your own.

Whenever cultures mix there are problems. It takes time and mutual trials to bring them together. Many of the Irish had been in the United States for twenty-five years. The country was not yet 100 years old. Only ten years before had we ended a conflict that threatened to tear us in two. It wasn't until a new stranger culture came to the United States that the Irish were no longer at the bottom of the social ladder. We have come a long way since then but have we learned the lessons of the past? Prejudice still exists today. Any time two different cultures interact. So how do we retain our culture without destroying each other? Education, understanding and tolerance. We do great things when we have a common enemy. We put all our differences aside and focus on the goal. My hope is that we can find the balance. Remember our cultures but focus on a future of understanding and tolerance.

Chapter One

Mahanoy City, July 1875

The fire raged in a hot swirling spiral. Flames licked the dark sky. Smoke and cinders blew in great circles around the brave volunteers on the ground as the heat singed their eyebrows. Sweat poured down their blackened faces leaving behind tiny tracks like white rivers. The smell of burning wood permeated the air to the extent that the taste lingered in the mouth. They could handle the smoke and the dirt, for it was not much different from the coal mines they worked in the day. However, this Saturday night would end in tragedy.

They had been fighting the fire for close to four hours now and everyone was showing their fatigue. Many of the worthy volunteers had been at their favorite taproom when the alarm was sounded even though most of their drinking was now based on the credit extended to them by the owners. The recent strike had taken its toll on their drinking and the barkeeps felt it too.

The Citizens Steam Fire Company Number 2 had their new Silsby, the "Lady Jane Smith," pumping from the creek with Ralph Lee manning the engine. They were the new company in town. Formed in

1870, just two years after the Humane Fire Company, by the disenchanted Welsh and English who couldn't stand the Irish who were taking over the Humane.

The Humane Fire Company Number 1 were hooked to Mr. Silliman's water company's new hydrants. Their hose cart completely empty.

Thank God for the rain the night before. The Mahanoy Creek flowed right through the center of town and provided a perfect source for water. The creek was running full and the Silsby was at full steam. The hoses were running this way and that, tangled in an intricate maze while the volunteers directed the streams on the blaze. The steam and smoke rose into the sky blotting out all the stars.

The Humane was set up on the east side and the Citizens on the west. The Citizens had a small sandbag dam set up and since they were downstream they were taking advantage of the runoff from the Humane's hoses upstream. The fire had started small enough, in the tool shed out back, but it was July and very hot and humid. The temperature had passed 100 that day. It was now about 80 and the wind was strong, the kind of night when you could expect thunder storms almost anytime. These conditions caused the fire to quickly spread to the house. The house was an Irish miner's house and his tool shed had powder for blasting as well as all the tools he needed to practice his trade.

The "Long Strike", as the six month long strike became known, was barely over and the mine owners were taking their good old time calling the miners back to work. Especially if your name was Irish. Michael Murphy was the first Irishman to become a miner in Mahanoy City, a town founded by Germans and English. The experienced Welsh miners moved in to mine the coal. They provided the skill. The Irish provided the labor. It was unheard of for an Irishman to become a miner. Miners worked under contract to the mine owners and paid their laborers directly. Mike worked hard and made it, but this fire would most likely ruin him. All his tools, all his investment was now gone.

The result of fire is always the same and now the Murphy family was homeless. Thank God everyone was safe. The dry wood burned like a bonfire and there was no one who could challenge its power and expect to win. The best they could do was to protect the nearby buildings. They turned their hoses on the buildings in an attempt to keep the fire from spreading. Even the Welshmen in the Citizen's were behaving themselves. It was just too hot for anyone to cause trouble.

As the fire burned down to its cinders and there was no more threat of its spreading, the inevitable occurred. One of the boys from the Citizen's lobbed the first rock over the back fence. He was probably a Modoc, the Welsh answer to the Molly Maguires. There were many gangs in the coal fields, most were clan oriented. The Mollies and the Modocs, the two most prominent gangs, accepted a wider group of members. For the Modocs you needed to be Welsh, for the Mollies you were Irish. Their hatred for each other was known throughout the region.

The rock struck Pat Casserly square in the back as he was rolling up hose in the yard. Pat was a very big man, 6'4", 240 pounds of Irish muscle. His flaming red hair was famous all over town. The rock wasn't near large enough to hurt him just large enough to get his attention. He was not the man to hit. He yelled out at the top of his lungs, "Those bastards have started it again lads. Let's finish this!"

The brawl was on. It was the third time in as many months. Each fire had been started in a small back shed and each fire ended in a street brawl. This time though the fire went too far and seven people were homeless.

Pat had been the foreman of the Humane for the past two years. He was well respected by all the men and was proving his leadership abilities almost daily. His Irish temper was his worst enemy and he worked very hard at controlling it. His father, Bernie, had taught him that violence was not the answer to a problem. He taught him to think, to be smarter than the next guy. "Use your head!" his dad used to say. This time was different. The only thing those protestant bastards understood was a thorough thrashing. After all, they started it. They probably started the fire too, since they didn't care for the fact that Mike Murphy had become a miner.

It was a real donnybrook. The fists flew. Pat was leading the pack with Big Mike Dugan on his left and Matthew Dougherty on his right. Mike Dugan was a veteran bare knuckles fighter and he showed it. Mike put three men down with his first three punches.

"That's the way to hit 'em, Mike," said Pat.

"I'll save the next one for you Pat," Mike replied.

Matthew, Pat's best friend, yelled, "Pat! Duck your head!" Just as a six-foot pike rounded over his head. It was wielded by Big Bill Jones, one of the Modocs. Matt picked up a broken ax handle and shoved the butt end into Jones' stomach. Jones doubled up and collapsed from his pain.

"Thanks for the warning Matt," yelled Pat. "I owe you one."

"Never mind that, Pat. Let's just get this done with."

Just then Pat felt a shrieking pain from his left shoulder right down to his feet. Jess Major, another one of the Modocs, had struck Pat from behind with a brass hose nozzle still attached to its hose. It temporarily caused Pat's left arm to go numb but his right arm was just fine. He turned and laid a solid right to the side of Jess's head knocking him out cold and collapsed next to Jess. As the feeling began to return to his left arm, he reached over to check on Jess. He was still breathing and Pat felt relieved. For a moment, he thought Jess was dead. Pat turned and walked away from the fight feeling totally disgusted with himself and the town he had chosen to live in. He had let his anger take over and almost killed a man. Why was there always a fight?

The fight wound down quickly, a hard days work, four hours of firefighting in ungodly heat followed by a good brawl was enough for any man. They quit more from exhaustion than anything else. No one really knew who won, although the battle would be relived many times in the next few weeks. It would have different versions each time and the outcome would depend on whether you were hearing it at the Humane's or the Citizen's. The *Mahanoy Valley Record*, Mr. Spenser's paper edited by John Parker, would give a fairer view of things. Of course Mr. Spenser was a friend of the working man and supported his right to organize and bargain for better treatment and wages. The *Mahanoy Gazette* would report that the Irish hooligan's had once again, through their ineptness, caused a home to burn. Then, showing their ignorant nature, started a fight when the facts of their ineptness were brought to their attention at the end of the fire. Milliam Ramsey would see to it. The *Gazette* had become the worst paper in town since Milliam bought it from Dr. Swayze back in '66. Tom Foster, at the *Shenandoah Herald,* would condemn the Irish as usual. Foster was bitterly against the Irish and had become a voice for the Philadelphia and Reading Railroad boss Franklin Gowen. Things had really heated up in the papers the past two weeks since the attempted murder of Bully Bill Thomas and the murder of a policeman in Tamaqua, Benjamin Yost

The men rolled the hose back onto the hose cart and picked up the rest of their axes and pikes and returned to the firehouse. After everything was readied for a swift departure, they headed home for some sleep.

It was almost 3:00 A.M. when Pat reached the house. His wife, Kate, greeted him with a kiss on the cheek. Not much was said as she helped him remove his shirt. She said nothing about the dried blood in his hair and down the side of his face. He took his seat at the kitchen table and rested his head in his hands. Kate wet a cloth in the bowl on the dry sink and began patting it on the side of his head where the blood had dried. He held his head up and she cleaned his face of the dried blood.

"I must look a holy mess," said Pat.

"Yes, but you're my holy mess and by God's grace I'll take care of you," said Kate. "Those Welshmen start trouble again, did they?"

"That they did," Pat said. "That they did. I am really getting tired of this fighting. I'm getting too old for this. If I'm elected president of the Humane I'll do everything I can to bring peace between us."

"Listen to yourself, Patrick. You'd think you were Robert Emmet. The English killed him before they would have peace."

"You can't compare me with Emmet. I have no desire to be a martyr. What was that he said before they hanged him?"

" He said, ' When my country takes her place among the nations of the Earth, then and only then, let my epitaph be written.' He wanted freedom and peace and all it got him was the noose. What makes you think you can make peace? They'll kill you too. They don't want Irish being more than their laborers. Even the southern slaves had it better. They were property and their owners took care of them. Here Irish laborers are treated like expendable resources. Every time an Irishman moves ahead they see to it that he takes two more steps back. Look what happened tonight. Do you really think the fire at Michael

Murphy's was an accident? They didn't want him back in the mines as a miner. They probably thought that if they destroyed his tools he would have to go back to laboring. Only it back fired and the whole house burned down. Not that they care. I'm sure they are just as happy with this result. It puts him back two steps instead of one. You know that somehow Monday's newspaper will try to blame the Molly Maguires, but the Ancient Order of Hibernians will be poor Michael's only hope for survival. I hear their benevolent fund is very large. How can the papers continue to lie? Why do they think we are so stupid as to believe that our own would hurt us in such a way, there is nothing to be gained by hurting our own kind. Freedom of the press without truth is useless. The English press are just trying to get us to fight with each other. Look at you Pat. You are all cut up because of them. They would have you burned out too if you cause them any trouble."

"Now Kate, calm down. You don't need to tell me about the English. I have no love for them either. The good Lord did not put us here to fight with each other. He knows I've fought all my life. First in Ireland, then in Philadelphia and now here. I just want some peace. My Pa and I left Ireland looking for a better life and so did you Kate. The famine killed my mother and sisters and the Philadelphia mobs killed

my father. I have to believe there is more here. I have
to believe that it is not Ireland all over again. No one
ever told us that we would have an easy life. Even the
wealthy have their share of problems. Theirs may be
different from ours, but problems none the less.
Somewhere, somehow this fighting has to stop. We
need to bring about mutual respect."

"Mutual respect? The mules in the mines get more
respect. The English only look for ways that we can
make more money for them. That's all they respect,
money. They are greedy, greedy people. They don't
want to share the wealth. They think they are better
than us and that we should keep quite and know our
place."

"Kate, I'm not asking that we all be wealthy. I just
think we should get fair wages and fair treatment. The
mines can't run without laborers and they deserve
more. There is no need for violence from either side.
I'm convinced that John Siney has the right ideas. His
union, the Workers and Laborers Benevolent
Association, says that organization and unity of cause
will succeed without violence."

"John Siney? He only brought six long months of
strife with his ideas. Besides he's off on bigger things
now. He has no more time for us. The mine owners
waited the men out. You could say they starved them
out. How can common working men hold out against

wealthy mine owners and large corporations? Frank Gowen and his railroad cronies used there own violence to break the strike. Now Gowen will bury Siney and his ideals. His union is broken and the casualties are all around us. Gowen and the mine owners won. Siney's strike failed."

"You're beginning to sound like Frank McHugh or Mike O'Brien and that Hibernian gang. They would have everyone a confirmed Molly. I hope to God they don't start up with their shenanigans. The strike's over and it's time everyone got back to work. Enough of this talk now let's get to bed. Father Ryan will be expecting us in fine shape for mass in the morning."

Chapter Two

Morning came quickly for Kate and Pat. It was another hot July day. The sky was clear and the sun was already heating up. The smoke smell hung in the air from the fire the night before, overpowering the aroma coming from the stove. Kate and Elizabeth were getting breakfast ready. Elizabeth was just eleven but she knew how to help mom. She set the table and then went to get Catherine and Michael ready for breakfast. Her older brother, Bernard, came down the stairs as she was leaving the kitchen. Bernard was named for Pat's father, Elizabeth for his sister and Kate for his mother. His sister and mother were both lost to the great famine.

"What's your hurry Lizzy?" cried Bernie. She hated when he called her Lizzy. She preferred her full name. She turned up her nose in disgust of her brother and continued up the stairs.

"Now Bernie, don't pick on her. She's my best helper," said Kate.

Bernard was fourteen and now a mule driver at the North Mahanoy Colliery. He had worked through the colliery as a breaker boy and then a door boy. He was a hard worker and took to the mules easily. Pat did not like the idea of him working in the mines but times were very hard since they left Philadelphia. They

needed all the money they could get. Pat did well in
Philadelphia making fine furniture for the rich. He
was able to save some money which was now getting
them through the strike. He left for the coal regions
because of the fighting and prejudice, because he
wanted a better life for his family. A new life in a new
town surely would be a fresh start.

Elizabeth woke the two little ones, Catherine was
eight and Michael was five.

"Come now you two get washed up for breakfast.
It's Sunday and the Lord doesn't want to see your dirty
faces." She sent the two of them out to wash and go
down to breakfast.

In a short time they were all seated and ready to
eat. Pat asked the Lord for a blessing and they began.
There wasn't much these days, only some bread and
strawberry jam that Kate had made up last month.
Money had been tight during the strike and the colliery
had just reopened this week. Bernie had just gone
back to work and wouldn't see a pay for another week.
Pat was a huckster and a carpenter and neither
business was good during the strike. He could sell no
goods since the miners had no money. His carpentry
work was cut almost to nothing because he was Irish.
Most of his carpentry work was for the English mine
superintendents. When the strike started they cut him
off as well. Never the less they still fared better than

the mine workers due to a few sympathetic German shop keepers who still gave him some work. Pat had many contacts with the local business people. These people kept him working with small jobs throughout the strike.

"All right now everyone, let's get ready for church," said Pat. "Father Ryan will not wait for us. You don't want him to be angry with us for being late."

Father Michael A. Ryan had not become known as a particularly patient man in his short time in Mahanoy City. He had come in March by special appointment of Archbishop Wood. People had wondered why the Archbishop would want to replace Father McFadden. McFadden had done so much at St. Canicus after Father McAvoy left. He raised the roof, erected the bell tower and placed that magnificent bell. He was a caring shepherd to his flock, knowing everyone by their first names. He was very successful and the parish had grown. It was quite odd to replace him without notice. There was a lot of speculation that Archbishop Wood was doing a favor for Franklin Gowen, President of the Philadelphia and Reading Railroad. Ever since the Reading Coal and Iron Company started to buy up all the mines it seemed as though many things had suddenly changed. The strike was just the beginning of the end for the union. The Molly Maguires, however, were still putting up a fight and Father Ryan was not about to stand for it. Father McFadden was sympathetic to their cause. He had seen first hand how the mine owners treated them. Father Ryan was fresh from St. Patrick's in Philadelphia, strongly influenced by Archbishop Wood.

Pat, Kate and kids stepped out onto Railroad St. and walked up to Catawissa St. on their walk to St. Canicus Church. The humidity was oppressive and everyone quickly became uncomfortable in the heat. They passed Reifsnyder and Yost's Lumber yard and then the Farmer's and Drover's Hotel on Center St. Young Michael started running ahead to catch up with his friend Martin Dougherty. Martin was the fifth son of Pat's good friend Matthew Dougherty. These were two close families, the Casserly's and the Dougherty's. Matt had married Mary Eagan several months before Pat and Kate were married. Matt was a laborer at North Mahanoy Colliery. His oldest son, Matthew Jr. was a mule driver there as well. The three middle sons Thomas, John and James, were breaker boys. Martin was only five and still three years from working at the breaker.

"Good morning Patrick, my old friend," said Matt Dougherty. " How's the family on this fine day? Quite a night we had, wasn't it?"

"That it was. That it was," said Pat. "I must say,

Mrs. Dougherty, you are looking fine this morning."
Pat always complemented the ladies, that's what made
him a good huckster.

"There is no need for your flattering talk on me
Patrick Casserly," she replied. "I'll not be buying
anything today." She knew him too long to be taken
in by his golden tongue.

"Well Mary, can't a man pay you a little
compliment without taking a tongue lashing?"

"Save your compliments for your paying customers,
Pat, no sense wasting them on the likes of me."

"You don't do yourself justice Mary. If I didn't
have such a fine woman in Kate I would have married
you myself."

Matt responded, "What makes you think she would
have had you when she already had me?"

"Now you two stop this now! Mary and I are not
going to listen to you two fools already this morning,"
yelled Kate. "I swear you two will never grow up.
You're like children."

When Kate Casserly spoke, people listened. These
two big Irishmen, who the night before held their own
in a street brawl, were no match for Kate. She knew
they were all talk.

"Now behave yourself before the Father sees you.
What kind of example are you setting for the boys?"

They walked up the steps of the church and were

greeted by Father Ryan.

"Good morning, Father," said Matt.

"Good morning, Mr. Dougherty. Have you given up the A.O.H. yet? I'm afraid you won't like what I have to say today."

"I'm sure I don't know what you're referring to Father. The A.O.H. is not something I'd be interested in. I am thinking of joining St. Patrick's Benevolent Association. Richard Gill has been talking to me about it."

"Good morning, Father," Pat interrupted. "Very tragic affair last night. Michael Murphy was a good man. He just made it to miner, too."

"Yes, Michael and his family have moved in with his sister, Margaret Foley and her husband Jim. He is strong and will make things work out. It's those Molly Maguires that are making things bad for us. If they would stop their shenanigans there would be less trouble for all. I'll have a few things to say to them today."

"I know you're right Father. My father taught me that violence was never the solution. I don't know how one is to get justice though. It just doesn't seem right the way the mine laborers are treated. The owners place more value on those mules than they do the poor souls that dig the coal"

"God will show us all justice Patrick. Just

remember your reward is with Him."

"Thank you Father. Come now children let's take our seats." Pat and family proceeded to their usual pew fourth row from the front on the right side. The Dougherty's sat right behind them.

Mass proceeded in its usual order except today there was an air of anticipation. Father Ryan had wanted a full house so he spread the word that he had a major announcement for this Sunday's sermon. The time had come and Father Ryan approached the pulpit. The parish grew silent as they awaited his blessing. He stood in the pulpit and surveyed his flock. He was careful to pause his gaze at all those he was told were Molly Maguires; intentionally making eye contact with each.

"In the name of the Father, Son and Holy Ghost," Father Ryan said as he administered his blessing.

The congregation all crossed themselves in response to his blessing and grew quiet in anticipation of his coming words.

"I stand before you today on this the ninth anniversary of St. Canicus Church as a representative of His Holiness Pope Pius IX in Rome and his servant the Archbishop of Philadelphia, James Frederic Wood; with the full authority of the Holy Church, a representative of our Holy Savior, Himself. I stand here filled with disgust in the way you have responded to His message of peace, of hope, of joy, of love and eternal life. For the past few months I have presented Christ's message to you. I have warned you of the dangers of these secret societies, these Molly Maguires. I have pleaded with you to turn these hoodlums over to the law to be dealt with in a manner fitting their atrocities. Yet you continue to ignore my pleas. You are a vile, sinful lot, worthy of eternal damnation.

"I have watched this community sink into Hell. Your greed and love of tobacco, whiskey and beer have dragged you to the brink of damnation. The Lord has delivered you here and provided for your care. He has given you work through these mines to provide food, clothes and shelter for your family. Just twenty-five years ago many of you were starving in Ireland. Your parents brought you here to start a new life. You have been given a new life through the kindness of the mine operators. And what is your response to your benefactor? You form labor unions, secret societies, all to undo what you have been given. You plot and scheme on new ways to destroy your life.

"You have just finished a six-month strike, aimed at destroying your employer and your livelihood. In that time you managed to destroy twelve breakers by fire, damaged countless pieces of equipment and gotten several people murdered. What makes you believe that the kindly people who provide the capital to operate these mines will want to continue to invest not only their time, but their money in these ventures when their generosity is repaid in such a manner as this? Nature brought on the potato blight and its resulting famine but this new famine you bring on yourselves. I cannot understand why Mr. Gowen and others like him insist on trying to save you from yourselves. The Reading Coal and Iron Company has seen fit to provide you with fair wages and housing for your families. For the first time you have a large company bringing in needed organization and capital to help you. Your repayment is to destroy their property."

The parish was silent as Father Ryan paused. Many searched the floor for a place to crawl into. The Mollies returned his looks defiantly. They saw their battle as a quest for justice. They fought with the only weapons they had, the same ones they had used for 700 years on the ould sod. They had to carry the fight for the timid, for they all knew what was right and just. All except Father Ryan it seemed.

Father Ryan resumed, "Last night, one of your brothers was burned out of his home. Why? What purpose did it serve? Michael Murphy is a fine man with a fine family. He is a hard worker. He received his reward by being promoted to miner. He showed his employer how grateful he was for his kindness. Yet Michael Murphy and his family were attacked.

Many say it was to get even for the brutal attempt to kill Bill Thomas. Others say it was because the Welsh don't want an Irish miner. I will tell you that either way, your greed and hatred has brought this on. If the evil men that lead these Mollies were brought to justice this revenge response would stop. You must abandon your foul methods. Even in the kindly act of fighting the fire, hatred and revenge dominate your thinking. The bloody brawl last night left several men unable to work, unable to provide food for their family. Lest you forget that last year our esteemed Chief Burgess, George Major, was shot to death while leading the Citizens Fire brigade in fighting a large blaze. Where is the cowardly perpetrator? He fled back to Ireland while Dan Dougherty faced the noose for him. These vicious acts will not be tolerated any longer. They cannot continue.

"I have told you many times of the Church's position on these secret societies. They are wrong in the eyes of God. The Pope, himself, has condemned them. Archbishop Wood has written many times against them. The newspapers across the land proclaim them a blight on decent society. Yet you protect them. Will not one of you step forward and identify the offenders?"

He paused again and searched for a response. None came.

"It pains my soul to say what I'm about to say. I will pray for your unfortunate souls. By the grace of our Lord and Savior will you be spared from eternal suffering. I hereby declare by the order of Archbishop Wood, Archbishop of the Diocese of Philadelphia, that all members of any secret societies, specifically the Ancient Order of Hibernians, Molly Maguires, Masons, Whiteboys, Ribbonmen, Odd Fellows or by any other name, are hereby excommunicated. They are cut off from the Church. They will receive no Holy Sacraments. You should not in any way associate yourself with any of these men less you yourself be corrupted by them and lose all your rights to the blessed sacraments. May God have mercy on their souls. In the name of the Father, Son and Holy Ghost, Amen."

The congregation was stunned. They had heard the warnings before but none believed the church would ever move to excommunication, the eternal damnation of their souls. Father Ryan stepped away from the pulpit and concluded the mass.

It was a slow somber walk home that day as everyone considered the consequences of the day's message. Even the children sensed the distress their parents felt. Distressed over what to do about what they knew. They had to deal with their fears of retribution should they come forward with information. There was nothing lower than an informer in Irish society. An informer would be ostracized for life. Worse than excommunication they would lose life as they knew it, better to face the unknown in death than to be banished from life.

That afternoon found Father Ryan in his study laboring over a letter to Archbishop Wood.

Your Eminence Archbishop Wood,

As was your desire, today I issued the excommunication of the secret society members, naming the organizations as directed. The reaction of the congregation was as I predicted. Not a single sole spoke. Greetings were exchanged upon dismissal from mass but no one gave me even a wink.

You may have been misinformed as to the names of the Mollies. During my sermon I intentionally looked them in the eyes and not one flinched. In the greetings afterwards, they remained cordial. This is either a very committed group of hardened criminals, or your sources are greatly disillusioned.

You sent me here to flush out the malcontents and see that justice is done. However, as each day passes, I find myself more confused by the issues. I have seen the laborers return from the mines each day. I have seen their children die. I have felt their sorrows. What justice am I here to seek? Never the less, I will flush out these murderers and thugs whoever they might be. Modoc or Molly, it makes no difference to me.

I am sure that my message will take some time to settle in. I will report my findings to you as soon as things are more evident. I will maintain my watch on O'Brien and McHugh. Possibly one of them will come forward. Frank McHugh is a devoted man and will do the right thing. I remain.

Your faithful Servant
Father Michael A. Ryan

St. Canicus Church

Chapter Three

"Philip's, three o'clock." William Major whispered to Big Bill Jones as they left the First Congregational Church. " Let the boys know."

"I'll be there," Jones responded.

"Good day, Mr. Major. How are things at the Citizen's?" said Pastor Lot Lake as he shook his hand. "How is that new hose cart working out?"

Frank Wenrich, councilman and chairman of the Police and Fire Committee, had gone to Philadelphia back in May to purchase a new hose cart to attend the new Silsby steam fire pump. Frank had also served as Chief Burgess before George Major.

"Why everything is just fine. We got a real work out last night," replied Will Major.

"So I've heard. When will those Irish stop starting all this trouble?"

"I don't know Pastor. I do know that the only education they understand has to be beaten into them."

"Now Will, you know that's not true. Some of them can be taught to drive a mule correctly."

"Yes but you still have to give them a hard knock on the head to get their attention. Good day to you Pastor."

Three o'clock came quickly and the Modocs began

to gather. John Hard had formed the Modocs in response to the Molly Maguires. They were all Welshmen and many had received a Molly coffin notice. They were meeting at Dave Philips' paper store on Center St. just east of Main. There was an entrance from Water St. next to the creek in the rear. Dave Philips sold books, stationary and all types of paper goods including blasting paper for making charges.

"Good afternoon, Jess. How's the head?" Dave said as he let Jess Major in the back door.

"Oh, I have a real headache today. I stopped at Hermany and Allen's Apothecary and got a headache powder. I had to get old John Allen to open up. It's a good thing he likes me so much. As for the fight, I'll get even with that Irish scum Casserly one way or another."

"Will is here and so is Bill Jones. Go right on in the others will be here soon."

Jess entered the back storeroom where Will and Big Bill Jones were seated at the table. Jones got up and bear hugged Jess.

"Well Jess, what a fight we had last night. I thought you got Casserly real good. He is one tough Irishman. Any other man would have been down for the count. I got to say I didn't expect to see you here today. He cracked you a good one."

"Why that motherless dog, he'll have his day. Where's Bully Bill?"

"Don't worry he'll be along any time. He don't move as fast since the shooting, especially since they killed his old mule instead of him. What they should've done was aim at the mule. They might have hit Bill then. The worst they could have done was that the old mule would have fell on him and killed him anyway," snickered Will.

"Enough of your bullshit, Will," Bully Bill said as he burst into the room. "I heard enough out of you. You ain't the one who was shot now are you?"

"You know, Jess and I barely made it out of Tuscarora. If that damn Donahue wasn't such a bad shot we both would be gone now. The bastard chased us for four hours before he gave up. I bet the county reps will give him a real bad time for not getting us clean. I think the Mollies are losing their edge after starving for six months. They couldn't even get one out of three of us."

"You can't talk about shooting straight. You're the one who missed Dan Dougherty and got us into this mess," cried Bill.

"All right, all right, you kids can fight another time, I got things to do today," John Hard said as he entered with Dave "Let's get this meeting started. Well kicking the Humane's ass was a hell of a way to get back at those Mollies. Whose idea was that anyway? By my tally, it was at best a draw. The best thing is that idiot Foster will tear them apart in the *Herald* tomorrow. We are no further ahead though. The mines are getting up to full speed again and the superintendents are starting to rehire the damn lowlifes. How the hell are we going to get rid of them? They're too stupid to move on no matter what we do to them."

"Now let's not go putting the blame on anybody. We all agreed that we could put a scare into them by burning out Murphy. The fight was just a little icing on the cake. Besides Murphy can't stay here now, he'll leave as soon as he can. I hear they're looking for miners up in Sugar Notch. If he's smart, he'll go quick," said Will. " Besides, if that damn superintendent lets him come back as a miner after this I'll shoot the son-of-a-bitch myself. They'll only blame it on one of the Irish anyway."

Jess interrupted, "Never mind all that. What are we going to do about Danny Dougherty? I don't give a damn about the rest of them but Danny Dougherty has got to go down and go down soon. I don't care what the jury said that bastard shot George and I want him dead."

"Why not let the Coal and Iron Police take care of it?" said John.

"The damn Coalies, what do you mean?" said Will.

"I mean we set him up. That shouldn't be too hard. Why a mule has a bigger brain than an Irishman."

"What's the plan?" said Jess.

"I have a few things to check out first. We'll get together next week and go over the whole thing. In the mean time, everyone on good behavior. Did you hear me Jones?"

"Good behavior?" said Jones. "I guess I can go a week without hitting an Irish."

"You better. We don't need any heat right now. Let the Irish stir the ashes now. See you next week, same time."

Now the Ancient Order of Hibernians usually hung out in Mike Flanagan's Saloon at 1st and Center or they were in a back room at the Merchant's Hotel at 2nd and Center. For really secure meetings they went to Mike Clark's house just up the street. James Duffy ran the Merchant's and was very sympathetic to the A.O.H. He was thinking about joining until Father Ryan made his little speech today. Now he wasn't sure he even wanted to let them in. He admired their ideals, the way they took care of each other. He was not sure why the Church would be so against Christian charity.

"Good afternoon, Mr. Duffy," cried Mike O'Brien

as he and Frank McHugh entered the lobby. "Are the boys here yet?"

"That they are, Mr. O'Brien, and be quick about your meeting, it's the last one you'll have here. I'll not associate with souls belonging to the Devil."

"You're not worried about what Father Ryan says are you? He's just doing what that scum Wood tells him to do. McFadden wouldn't play his game and now he's gone. You know Wood and Gowen are just trying to get more out of us. Gowen says jump and Wood says how much do I get? We saw enough of that on the ould sod. The priests kissing the English's ass just to get a favor. Besides, you can't excommunicate members of something no one can prove exits now can you?"

"You can't fool God, O'Brien. He knows what you are up to and he will send you straight to hell."

"Duffy, you think like an old women. You can't believe God is on the side of the English? And if not on the side of the English then surely He is with us. You wouldn't want to go against a holy mission now would you?"

"You're a hard man O'Brien. Get in the back before someone sees you here."

Mike O'Brien was the bodymaster of the A.O.H and Frank McHugh was the secretary. They held the power and they made the decisions. Mike and Frank walked down the corridor and opened the door to the back room hoping to have a few drinks and talk about the fire and the fight last night.

"Well!" Mike exclaimed, "James McKenna. Did they finally kick you out of Shenandoah?"

"Not in your wildest dreams, O'Brien. If that happened, I would go much farther than this filthy place," replied McKenna, secretary of the Shenandoah Chapter of the A.O.H. "How are you O'Brien? I heard you had quite a donnybrook last night with those damn Modocs again."

"Yes it was. Those bastards burned out a fine Irish family too. They need more than a beating, Jimmy. When are we going to be able to get even? I've had my fill with Jess and Will Major, and that Bully Bill Thomas is the most revolting of them all. When are we going to get them for trying to kill Danny Dougherty?"

McKenna looked at him with a stern eye. "You know I and three of my best men tried to kill Thomas. Hurley, Doyle and Gibbons were here on the fourth to take care of him. How were we to know half the county would be here trying to shut down Webster Colliery? With the state militia in town and all them Coalies what did you expect us to do? I had no choice but to put it off. You know we all want it to be a clean job. Then I sent Hurley, Gibbons and Morris who botched it. They swore to me that they had done a clean job. You give me no choice but to try again. I'll send five men next week. This time they'll get it right."

"I'll hold you to that McKenna or you'll get no more jobs from me," O'Brien responded angrily.

"I'll buy you a drink to seal the deal, Mike. Are you up to it?"

"When have I not been up to a drink with a friend? Frank, get the bar keep in here we need a round of drinks on Mr. McKenna here."

Just then Matt and Dan Dougherty entered along with Patrick McKeever.

"Welcome boys," yelled Mike. "You're just in time for a round of drinks on our friend Mr. McKenna."

"Thanks a lot Jim, but what about them Modocs? They gave us trouble again last night. When are we going to have justice for my brother Dan? Don't you think he has waited long enough?" Matt Dougherty was getting a little anxious at the site of McKenna. He knew he was John Kehoe's right hand man and Kehoe was the real power in the county.

"Now don't worry Matt. I just told Mike I'll send five men over next week. By that time things will have gotten quiet again. I don't want anyone hurt and I don't need all them Coalies and militia around either."

"That's fine with me, Jimmy. That Billy Bull and

those Major boys have got to be put it in their place."

"You know you guys could use a few more members in this group. What have you done about recruiting new members?" asked McKenna.

Matt responded, "I guess they didn't tell you about Father Ryan's little sermon today. It will be awful hard to grow the ranks now that the church has excommunicated us all."

"No, they didn't tell me," said McKenna. "What are you going to do now? Is everyone going to remain loyal to the oath? We can't have no stinking squealers now. Things are going bad enough."

Mike O'Brien butted in, "Don't you worry, they'll be no squealers in our group. Don't' worry about membership either. I'm the bodymaster here and our ranks will be growing much larger real soon. I got Pat Casserly ready to come over to our side. When Pat comes he'll bring about thirty of the Humane with him."

"You're talking out your ass, Mike. You'll not get Pat Casserly to come over, especially after Father Ryan's sermon. You know how Pat is with the church. He'll never defy Father Ryan."

"Defy him he will. I guarantee it. I'll tell you the plan just as soon as I get my final details together. Now let's drink on our good friend Mr. McKenna," Mike raised his glass. "May you be in Heaven a half hour before the Devil knows you're dead."

They all raised their glasses to the toast and drank. "What brought you here today, Mr. McKenna?" asked Dan Dougherty.

"I'm on my way to Philadelphia to see my sister. She said some men from Buffalo were nosing around and asking questions about me. I want to reassure her that things are going well with me. I wanted to stop here on the way and tell you boys the plan to take care of Thomas."

McKenna stopped to give himself an alibi. He was really an undercover Pinkerton detective. He was going to Tamaqua to investigate the murder of policeman Benjamin Yost. McKenna's real name was James McParlan and he had infiltrated the Ancient Order of Hibernians in Shenandoah where he had become a secretary and a trusted member.

"Well off with you then. The train will be leaving shortly," replied Mike O'Brien.

McKenna stepped out of the room and made for the station. He would be in Tamaqua within the hour.

"OK, boys. Now let's get down to business. First things first, I vote we give Murphy $25.00 from the benevolent fund. All those in favor?"

They all responded with aye. One of the prime missions of the A.O.H was charity. They were the only safety net for most of the Irish.

"So be it then. Frank see that he gets the money today. Next on the agenda, what are we going to do about the rest of the Modocs. I don't want any more of us burned out. We have to stop them." O'Brien was fishing for ideas. He knew the A.O.H wouldn't survive much longer with the way things were going lately and he needed something to spark things up. The Yost murder in Tamaqua had started a backlash from the general public. They were ready to take matters into their own hands. Vigilance committees were meeting all over the coal region. The newspapers continued to put all the blame on the Molly Maguires. They equated all Irish as lowlife murderers. They fueled the formation of the vigilance committees.

"We need more members," cried McKeever. "We need people who aren't afraid to fight for justice. Matt, we really need Casserly? He fights with the best of them and is well respected."

"Casserly is not about to join us. I have been working on him for many years. He just doesn't think we can win by fighting. His father worked for the English back in Cork. He was the finest cabinet maker in the county and the English loved his work. They took good care of him while they used him. He was too dumb to see that they paid him only a pittance of what he was worth. His furniture sold for ten times the amount they paid him. He just couldn't see how they were using him. Pat's no different. He works his hands bare working for these stinking Germans and English. He can't see past his nose. He'll never see justice from the English any more than we will. You saw what they did to him during the strike. They cut him off just 'cause he was Irish. He starved with the rest of us. It was only a few that helped him at all."

"Calm down now Matt," said Mike. "Maybe McKeever doesn't have such a bad idea at that. Maybe Casserly just needs a little push? I told you I have a plan. What if we pressured him in a way that made it look like the Modocs were trying to get him? Then he would turn to us for help. He would bring an army to our side. Just what we would need to eliminate those bastards once and for all."

"Careful Mike," said McHugh. "I don't like the idea. It's not what we're about working against our own kind."

"Don't go soft on me now Frank. I need to get this group back on its feet before things get any worse around here. I don't like what the papers are saying about the vigilante groups forming. It's one thing to beat the noose with good alibis, it something else to face bullets from an angry mob. We need the respect that Casserly can bring us and we need the support of the men who will follow him. I just need a few more things to fall in place and he'll come running to us."

In the mean time in the back of Frank Wenrich's butcher shop another clandestine meeting was being held. Frank had been the Chief Burgess before George Major and now he was the chairman of the police and fire committee.

"Well gentlemen, I'm looking for ideas. The Irish are getting out of hand. Another fire last night and then a street brawl. Maybe we should just disband the Humane and only have one fire company. I guess I would have to file a court complaint and have their charter revoked. We need to do something to stop all the violence. It's a sad state of affairs when the governor has to send in the militia to keep peace. It is our job to control our town. We cannot let this go on any longer." Frank looked to the group for a response but was met with blank stairs.

"I understand that Father Ryan excommunicated the villains at mass this morning. That will only give them more resolve. We need to get ready to defend our property. I think we should form a vigilance committee or maybe our own militia. We can't stand by and watch all our work be burned down around us by a few thugs."

"Frank, I have never seen you so angry. Please calm down. We can work this out." The voice of Edward Silliman was heard over the crowd. "We need to do this right and within the law. I will support the idea that we form our own militia. I will provide the initial uniforms and rifles. We just need to get Governor Hartranft to issue a charter to become a part of the Pennsylvania Guards. That should be no problem since he is getting tired of sending troops here. What do you say Frank?"

"That's a very generous offer Ed. I think our own guard company is just what we need. I'll be the first to sign on. It's still going to take some time though. What do you think about starting a night patrol right now?"

"OK, that will give us some time to get things straight with the governor. Let's get organized."

Just then the door burst open and in walked Robert J. Linden, Captain of the newly formed flying squadron of the Coal and Iron Police, Chief of the Coalies. The unit had been formed to provide rapid response to trouble areas. They had their own steam engine and custom rail car to move them quickly about. They were greatly feared by all since they did not answer to the elected law. They only answered to Frank Gowen.

"Well Captain, what brings the Coal and Iron Police to my shop on a Sunday?" asked Frank.

"I might ask you what brings a group like this together on a Sunday? I don't see the minister so I don't think it's a prayer meeting," responded Linden.

"Enough sparing, Captain. What do you want?" interrupted Ed Silliman.

"The word on the street is that there is a citizen's vigilance committee being formed. You folks wouldn't know anything about that would you?"

"Captain we're all just as interested in seeing justice done as you are. We have gotten together to discuss the Irish problem and we think we have the answer," replied Frank. "Go ahead Ed, tell him our plan."

"I'm not interested in your plan. I'm here to tell you I won't have any amateurs getting in my way. I'll deal with the Irish scum. I don't need any help from you. My men are edgy enough and are ready to shoot anything out of the ordinary. I don't want any do gooders getting themselves shot. I'm warning all of you. Stay out of the way." He turned and slammed the door behind him.

Everyone in the shop stood silently in awe of Captain Linden. Was he suggesting that he would shot them? He surely was a powerful man in a powerful position. They were not expecting to have a problem with the Coalies. They all assumed that the Coal and Iron Police would welcome them with open arms. No one thought there would be any resistance.

"That man is an ignorant son of a bitch and I don't trust him," cried Ed Silliman. "Any true policeman would have listened to us and not jumped to conclusions. Our plan of forming a militia is a good sound plan. After all, we are just interested in peace and justice."

Sunday afternoon also brought together the members of the Humane at their picnic grove on the north side of town known as Smith's Farm. Here, since 1868, they held their annual picnic and preparations were now well underway for next Saturday's big event. Although the Humane was founded by the prominent citizens of the town who were mainly Americans of German descent, it had over the last few years become predominantly Irish. It had only taken two years for most of the original founders to leave and form the Citizen's Steam Fire Company and since then there has not been any peace. Only a few originals were still hanging around.

M. M. Ketner became the second president of the Humane in 1868 right after Fred Spiegel. This was a time when the company was predominantly German. Over the years as the Irish moved into the town to work in the mines they joined the Humane as well. Many of the Irish were now getting tired of Ketner's leadership. He seemed to them to be very arrogant especially since no one knew his first name. He always went by M. M. This forced everyone to call him Mr.

Ketner. He did still hold the respect of many however, since he was also Justice of the Peace.

Ketner walked onto the picnic grounds amidst a throng of eager workers busy with preparations for next Saturday's picnic. Pat Casserly and his son Bernie were hard at work on the bar. It needed extra special attention to handle the coming event. They did not want it breaking down under any circumstances. This is where most of the money would come in.

Patrick Dillion and John Quinn were in charge of the food. They were busy setting up their large tent and the stoves and ovens they would need. Even Dr. Phaon Hermany was there to help. Dr. Hermany was the original treasurer and now at age 33 he was also the coroner. He was also a partner in the Allen and Hermany Apothecary on Center St. There was also a stage for the band and a large area for dancing.

Ketner walked over to Pat Casserly saying, "Well Pat, your son is sure getting big."

"That he is, Mr. Ketner. He's a fine lad who works hard. I just hope I can get him to come out of those mines and work with me," Pat replied.

" I see you are teaching him your trade. Does he have the talent? Will he be as good as you?"

"He's still a little rough but he's getting better all the time. He needs to put in a little more practice and he needs to learn patience first. You can't be a good carpenter if you rush your work."

"Pat, if you can't teach him, no one can. Pat, I'm a little concerned. The word has it that you want to run against me for president of the fire company. Is this true?"

"True it is sir. I don't feel you have done enough to stop the fighting with the Citizens. We need to have peace before someone else gets killed because of this constant bickering and brawling."

"I suppose you think that you can change things."

"That's right I think I can. I know one thing for sure, I'll work at it much harder than you have, Ketner. I won't rest until we have peace and can work together."

"Well Pat, I'm only the second president that this company has had and there are still many Americans left who support me. You Irish have not taken over yet. I'll get all my votes here. You'll not stand a chance. I will stay here long after you are gone. My only goal is to survive all this nonsense and see that the Humane stays together. I can't be concerned about those malcontents, the Citizens. It's the damn Modocs and Mollies that cause all the trouble. How are you going to change them? Those Modoc Welshmen are no better than you Irish, you both like to drink and you both like to fight. I can't change your natures."

"Well-said Ketner. But you can't keep the company together without dealing with the Citizens problem. This fighting will tear us apart. You are not Irish, Ketner. You don't understand us. These men need a strong leader, one that can make them listen to reason. I feel they will listen to what I have to say and they will follow me. Most of these men have been persecuted all their lives. They don't know any other way but to fight. The English have kept us down trodden for over 700 years. Now in America we can finally be free men. These men must be taught the right ways. They must be taught how the law works. They must learn how to deal with people within the law. I will show them the way."

"You're a damn fool Casserly. They will turn on you at the first opportunity. They don't know what loyalty is. They can all be bought."

"Well, Ketner, only time will tell. In the mean time I have decided I will run against you. We will see in December who they want."

"Casserly, good luck to you. You'll need it. I'm a tough fighter. Let's get back to work we have a picnic to put on."

Chapter Four

Monday morning started promptly at five with Kate calling up the steps to Bernie. The Casserly household was always on time thanks to Kate. She had been up since four. The clothes were laid out for each child. Pat and Bernie's work clothes were ready. Breakfast was on the stove and Bernie's lunch was in his pail. She always tried to have some hard tack and bread along with tea. Sometimes she even added some carrots. Bernie would feed them to his mule for a treat. Pat would take a lunch with him for the day if he was going to be away. If he was staying in town he would try to have lunch with Kate. It was the only time of the day they could be alone together.

Today Pat would need his lunch too. He was off to Pottsville to see what he could find to sell from his cart. The mines were working again and the town folks would need to have the things that they had done without for so long. He really knew how to treat the ladies. He would always have something extra for them, some cloth for a dress, a new hat, and he knew how to get them to buy it. Pat hated the huckster side of his life. He much preferred being a carpenter. His father had taught him well and he loved doing it. The strike had hurt him but not as much as a mine laborer. He could not hide his Irish heritage and when the strike started the signs went up at every place of employment, "IRISH NEED NOT APPLY." Pat's carpentry work was severely cut. Only a few loyal customers, mostly Germans, helped him through. He had a large hand cart that he used to haul his lumber and tools. It made a perfect cart to display his goods while huckstering between carpentry jobs.

"Off to work with you now Bernie," Pat said as he handed Bernie his lunch. "Be sure to be careful with that mule today. As soon as things get back to normal around here and I start getting some carpentry work I'll need a helper. Then you can say good-bye to the God awful hole and work for yourself, be your own boss. You'll get some respect when you can provide for yourself. You won't have to be dependant on that superintendent's whims."

"I'll be careful Dad. Stay away from the Modocs today. They got enough of a beating yesterday."

"Don't you concern yourself with those Modocs. Soon they and the Mollies will be gone and we will finally get peace. Justice will find them. Whether it's God's justice or man's justice, it will surely take care of them. Now off with you boy, you'll be late."

Kate was busy getting the rest of the children ready for school. They had a long walk up to Spruce Street School and would spend their day with their teacher Mary J. McHugh. Miss McHugh started teaching in 1866 at the age of 13. She loved the children and loved to teach.

"Kate, I need to leave now or I'll miss the train to Pottsville."

"Pat, my love, you have a safe trip. You'll be back on the late train around 8:00 is that right?"

"Yes Kate. Please don't save supper for me I'll get something in Pottsville before I leave."

"Please be careful Pat. Watch out for those Major brothers and that crazy Thomas fellow. I don't trust any of them. If they find out your traveling they'll try to get you and your money."

"I'll be fine Kate. No one knows I'm leaving today. I'll be there and back before you know it. Have Bernie bring the cart to the station tonight so I can bring everything back. I want to sell it all by Friday so we can have a good time at the Humane picnic on Saturday."

Pat gave Kate a big hug and a kiss and left for the train station.

"Come children you must get ready to leave for school." Kate said with half a tear in her eye. She was very worried about Pat and the Modocs.

Bernie was not on the street long until his good friend Matt Dougherty, Jr. came running up behind him and laid his arm around his shoulder.

"Bernie, what's your hurry this morning?"

"Matt, you're always late and I'll not let you make

me late too."

"Bernie you worry too much. That old superintendent Garrett needs us or the coal will never make it to the shaft."

"Don't be an idiot Matt. We could get run over by our mules today and they'll have a new breaker boy driving them tomorrow."

"Not if we stick together. This strike almost broke them. We just needed to stay out a little longer. But no, we gave in just in time for them to start a new stock pile in Philadelphia. I guess you're right we are all idiots."

"Idiots with a pay now," said Bernie.

"Hey, I hear your dad set old Jess Major on his ass at the fire the other night?"

"I'm sure he deserved it. My dad wouldn't hit him if he didn't deserve it."

"Deserved it! Sure he deserved it. My dad said that he is one of the Modocs. He says the Mollies will get him soon and show him Molly justice."

"What do you know about the Mollies? You heard what Father Ryan said on Sunday. They have all been condemned to hell."

"I know that Father Ryan is too close to Archbishop Wood. My dad says that Wood is a servant of Frank Gowen. He says Wood would do anything for Gowen as long as he gets what's his.

Gowen is out to use all of us for his gain. The only way to fight back is with Molly justice."

"Well my dad says that Molly justice is wrong. He says that God has given man the power of justice and that justice is from the law."

"You can't believe that. The law is Gowen's law. He controls the law. Hell, in Mahanoy City, he is the law. What do I have to do to convince you to come over to the Molly way? I can show you what justice is all about."

"I'm not sure Matt. What you say makes sense. But what about my dad? He would skin me alive if I became a Molly. You may be right, but I'm just not sure. I need to know more. I can't have my dad find out."

"That's why they call it a secret society Bernie. No one will know you are a Molly."

"Maybe so. Let me think about it."

"Casserly and Dougherty." screamed Nathan Garrett, mine superintendent. "Get over here now. You're both late. Serves me right for bringing you Irish back to work. I should have known better than to think you shiftless bastards could be on time."

"We're sorry Mr. Garrett," said Bernie. "It won't happen again."

"It had better not happen again, Casserly or you'll both be out of work. Now get to work!"

Bernie and Matt hopped into the coal car and within seconds they were on their way to the bottom of the shaft. They each made their way to the stable area to get their mules and head off to start hauling the coal cars to the shaft. Matt worked the east gangway and Bernie the west. As Matt started into the east gangway, he was approached by a large dark figure, Mike O'Brien.

"Well young Matt. Did you have a talk with Bernie Casserly as I asked?"

"Yes, Mr. O'Brien. I did and I think he is listening and coming around. He is starting to doubt that his father is right. I'm just not sure what will turn him over to us."

"You've done fine lad. I'll handle it now. You go on about your business."

O'Brien had set the hook in the first part of his plan to get Pat Casserly in the Mollies and now he needed to real the fish in, or was Bernie just the bait? No matter, he needed a way to get at Pat and using his son seemed most appropriate.

Mike headed for the west gangway. "I need to show young Casserly how Gowen's justice works." Mike thought to himself. "I'll get him in a little trouble with Garrett. That just might do the trick. I'll need a little powder and a tin cup."

It wasn't hard finding Casserly and his mule. They

were hooked up and starting to pull a car back to the shaft to be lifted to the breaker.

O'Brien found a cut in the tunnel wall and pushed himself back into it to await young Casserly. He was on the opposite side with the mule between him and Bernie. As the mule approached he held out the tin cup, which had about a quarter inch of black powder in the bottom and dropped in his cigarette. A blinding white flash blew up right in front of the mule's eye causing him to bolt right into Casserly and the side wall. The force being sufficient enough to derail the car and spill coal all over the gangway. O'Brien fled toward the shaft to get Mr. Garrett.

"Garrett, Garrett," cried Mike O'Brien. "There has been an accident in the west gangway. Come quickly."

Nathan Garrett took off down the gangway to see what the problem was. It was his job to see that the coal kept moving. No matter what.

"O'Brien, did you see what happened?" Garrett asked.

"Well I was just ahead when I heard the noise. I looked back and saw Casserly and the mule heading to the wall and the coal starting to spill out. It looks like Casserly got knocked out in the process."

Just as Garrett and O'Brien arrived, Bernie was shaking the cob webs loose from his head.

"Casserly, what in the hell did you do? You've

spilled my coal all over and derailed the car. Get your ass up and get out of my mine. I won't have any more of your problems. O'Brien, get a crew here now and clean this mess up."

"Yes sir, Mr. Garrett, right away sir," said O'Brien.

"Mr. Garrett, sir. Can I explain?" said Bernie.

"What's to explain? You spilled my coal all over the gangway. Mr. Gowen will have my hide if production slips. Get out of my mine before I lose my temper."

Bernie walked away and headed for the shaft. "So that was Gowen's justice," he thought to himself. "I didn't even get a chance to tell him the mule was spooked by a flash of light. It must have been from a charge, but I really didn't think I was close to any. I wonder what really did happen? Well, Matt was sure right. You can't get any justice when Gowen is in control. I'll get justice. I'll get Molly justice."

The walk home was a long one for Bernie. What would he say to his mother? What would he say to his father? He really let them down. The family needed all the income they could get. Now he had let them down.

"Bernie, are you all right? Are you hurt? Why are you home so early?" said Kate as Bernie came into the kitchen.

"I'm OK Mom. There was an accident in the

mine."

"Oh my God is anyone hurt?"

"No Mother, it was my accident. I had a problem with my mule and he upset a car of coal. I'm really not sure what happened, everything went so fast. I think I saw a bright flash but it must have been caused by my head hitting the side wall. I was knocked out and don't remember any more."

"My poor baby let me get a cold cloth for your head."

"It was really awful. When I came around, Mr. Garrett was over me yelling about how I spilled his coal all over his mine. He wouldn't even let me explain. He just fired me. He told me to get out of his mine before he lost his temper. I guess I am a real disappointment to you. I'm very sorry I let you down."

"Don't be silly Bernie. It wasn't your fault. Those mines are dangerous places and accidents happen. Mr. Garrett had no right to not listen to you. He is not a fair man. Well let's get you cleaned up. I want you to rest until it's time to take the cart to the station for your father."

"OK mother, I'll rest and I will tell father what happened tonight. Do you think he will be ashamed of me?"

"Your father could never be ashamed of you no

matter what you did. Rest now."

After supper Bernie got the cart ready to go, he did not want to be late. He pushed it to the station and got there just minutes before the train pulled in. The sun was setting in a brilliant red and orange sky as the big steam engine pulled into the station. Bernie loved the smell of the sulfur and the oil from the big engine. He often wondered if he could be an engineer. That, he knew, was impossible. He was Irish. What he didn't know was that he was being watched. Jess Williams and Bully Bill Thomas were also at the station.

"There's Casserly's young lad with his dad's cart," Jess said to Bully Bill. "Casserly must be on the train and bringing some goods back to sell."

"Let's teach him a lesson he won't forget," said Bully Bill. "That Irish bastard caused you a lot of pain and embarrassment. We can get him and his kid if we surprise them."

"OK Bill, here's what we'll do. Casserly will unload his stuff into his cart and will go straight down Railroad Street back to his place. There is a place we can hide just below where the cribbing ends about a block down. We'll take them there. Do you have your gun in case we need it?"

"I won't need a gun on him. I'll take him with my bare hands," boasted Bill.

"Don't underestimate him Bill. He is a very powerful man. My head still aches," cautioned Jess.

"You take care of the kid and leave Casserly to me. Let's go."

Pat got off the train as it stopped and Bernie greeted him. The train was a little early but Bernie had made it in time.

"Hi Pop. Did you have a good trip?" Bernie said with a forced smile.

"Yes I did, Bernie. I have lots to sell this week." Pat sensed that something was wrong. Bernie was acting strange, kind of fidgity. "What's the problem Bernie?"

"How did you know there was a problem?"

"I just sensed it lad. Now tell me what happened. Is everyone all right?"

"Yes, everyone is fine. The problem is with me Pop. I let you and Mom down. I had an accident at the mine today. My mule bolted and the coal car spilled all over the track. Mr. Garrett fired me. I'm really sorry. I will find another job right away. I'll start looking . . . "

Pat interrupted, "Calm down lad. I am not disappointed in you. There is nothing to be sorry for. Garrett's not the kind of man to get upset over. He cares nothing about anything if it don't line his pockets. All things happen for good you know.

Maybe it's time you joined me. The carpentry work
will be picking up soon, that damned strike held
everyone back. People just need time to get back on
their feet. I'll hear no more about this now. You and
I are partners and that's it. Let's get this cart loaded
and get home. We'll have a big day tomorrow."

"OK Pop I'll work hard for you, you'll see."

Pat and Bernie went to the baggage car and started
to unload all the things that Pat brought back from
Pottsville. Over the years he had made lots of friends
in Pottsville, each willing to extend him credit. He had
new pots and pans, bolts of cloth, some new brooms,
pails, and scrub brushes. He even found a hat for old
Mrs. Haughney. Her grandson was getting married
next month and she asked Pat to bring her something
nice. There were many other merchants in town but
Pat sold to the Irish and always at a better price.
Sometimes he extended credit far beyond what he
should have but no one ever failed to pay him back.
Now, with his new partner, it would be more
important than ever to get some carpentry work, that
is what really paid the bills.

Bernie and Pat finished loading their hand cart and
they both took a handle and started pushing the cart
home. They turned off Main Street and started down
Railroad Street which was just an alley behind the main
business section. Although it was still light, the sun

was setting fast, it was just ready to drop behind the distant hills when Jess Major and Bully Bill Thomas struck. Thomas let the first blow go to the back of Pat's neck. It was a two-handed punch that sent Pat to his knees. Just seconds later Major swung a large stick that he had found laying by the cribbin' across the back of Bernie's legs bringing him to the ground as well.

The beating progressed without mercy. Thomas caught Pat with a kick to the stomach and a second two fisted blow to the back of the neck. Major threw a right hand into Bernie's side and followed with a kick to the side of his head. Just then a shot rang out from on top of the railroad bank. Jess and Bill looked up and saw Captain Linden and two of his officers.

"Jesus Christ Jess, it's the Coalies. Run!" screamed Thomas.

Jess and Bill took off down Railroad St. with all that they had left.

"Shall we go after them Captain?" cried one of the Coalies.

"No leave them go. I don't want to get involved with their gang wars. I'm only concerned with keeping the property of the Philadelphia and Reading safe. That's our job. Besides that it's only a couple of Irish. They'll heal. Let's get back to the train."

Captain Linden and his two officers walked back

up the tracks to the train, leaving Pat and Bernie in the street.

By now several people came running from Center St. responding to the shot. Frank Wenrich was in the crowd. They found Pat and Bernie beginning to stir.

"Pat, are you OK?" Wenrich inquired. "Someone help me get him up and get the boy too."

"I'll be all right." Pat responded. "How's Bernie? Did anybody see who it was?"

"I'm OK Pop," replied Bernie. "What happened?"

"We were ambushed by someone, probably Modocs or some other thieves. I can't say for sure I didn't see them. Where's the cart?"

"Your cart's right here Pat," said Wenrich. "It looks pretty full. Where did the shot come from?"

"Shot? What shot? I didn't hear a shot," Pat replied.

Wenrich said, "That's what brought all of us here. We heard a gun shot. It must have scared your attackers away."

"I sure am grateful to whoever fired that shot," Pat said as he examined his cart. "Everything seems to be here. I better get the lad and this stuff home before they decide to come back."

"I'll walk with you," Wenrich said. "You live just below Catawissa, right?"

"Yes Mr. Wenrich, that's right. Thank you so

much for your concern. I wish everyone cared as much as you do. Maybe we could get some peace in this town."

Frank Wenrich accompanied Pat and Bernie home and waited until they had unloaded their cart.

"Thanks again, Mr. Wenrich," said Pat as he shook hands.

"Think nothing of it Casserly. Good luck to you." Wenrich walked back to Center St. and back to his home.

Kate met them at the door.

"What in God's name happened to you two. Are you hurt?"

"Our pride more than anything. We were attacked as we came down from the station. Apparently an attempted robbery. Neither Bernie nor I got a look at them. It could be the Modocs though. They are awfully mad about the beating they took at the fire on Saturday," Pat replied as he gave Kate a big hug. "It's gettin' very late, we've all had a long day. Let's get to bed and we can discuss this more in the morning."

Chapter Five

Saturday came fast that week as Bernie worked with Pat to sell all the goods that he brought back from Pottsville. Bernie was a fast learner. He watched his dad's way with the women and picked up quickly on how to talk to them. Pat was always a gentleman but with a little bit of the devil in him. He knew how to be polite and exciting at the same time. He really had the gift of the blarney stone. Bernie picked it up with ease. Why, Bernie was even able to sell old Mrs. Haughney the hat they got "just for her." They had been very fortunate this week as well. Mr. Abraham Focht, president of the First National Bank, had asked Pat to do a major addition at his house. It was enough work for him and Bernie to last until December. They would have plenty of money to get through the next winter.

There was a big problem though. Bernie was filled with anger. He hated Nathan Garrett for firing him like that. Garrett was just another of Frank Gowen's henchmen and somehow Bernie knew he would get even. Today, however, was a day of fun. Each evening the whole week they had gone to the Humane Picnic grove to get things ready for the big annual picnic. They had sold enough during the week to see that everyone had a ticket and the whole family would

be going. The Humane had been very successful this
year in getting donations and were able to drop the
ticket price to twenty-five cents. Mr. Kaier was so glad
the strike was over he had donated all the beer. He
needed to celebrate too. The long strike had hurt
everyone deeply and it was time to celebrate the return
to work. There had been enough sorrow and
suffering.

The Casserly household was filled with excitement
as were all of the Irish houses in town. It was picnic
day and everyone was getting ready for a day of fun
and celebration.

"Elizabeth!" cried Kate. "You need to sit on
Michael and get him calmed down or we'll never be
ready to go. Michael! You settle yourself or we'll leave
you at home."

"Kate, don't be too hard on the lad, he's just
excited," Pat remarked. "Catherine, can you help your
sister with Michael?"

Catherine was very quiet usually. Bernie always
dominated the scene since he was the oldest.
Elizabeth was always helping Kate. Michael was the
baby and seemed to always need attention. She always
felt a little lost. Pat recognized this and always tried to
give her something to do when times got a little tense.
She was really Pat's favorite.

"Sure daddy, I can get Michael to calm down,"

Catherine answered.

Bernie was already out on the street pacing. He hated when they he had to wait for the whole family. After all he would soon be fifteen, shouldn't he be able to go on by himself. After all he held a job in the mines and now was his dad's partner, he was an adult. Why did they still treat him like a child? Why did he need to wait?

Well it took another twenty minutes but Kate finally had her family in order. She was satisfied that all were presentable and they could leave for the picnic. It was eight o'clock and breakfast was being served from six to ten to accommodate all those who slept a little later than usual. They still had a half hour walk to get to Smith's Farm where the Humane had held its annual picnic for the last seven years and it was sure to be the biggest, most exciting picnic ever. The walk to Smith's Farm that morning looked like a St. Patrick's Day parade. If you were Irish, you were there. That's not to say that others weren't invited too. Many of the town's Americans also came. Most of them were Pennsylvania German entrepreneurs who made up most of the merchant class of the town. After all it was good for business. The politicians came too. They had come to respect the power of the Irish vote and came to show their support, although many of them secretly loathed the Irish, but politicians haven't changed much since Caesar's time.

They arrived at Smith's Farm about 8:35 and it was already very full. The food stands were very crowded as people lined up for breakfast. Families were vying for tables. Most had sent someone early to get a desirable table. The Casserly's were content with any table at all. They got in line for breakfast and Matt Dougherty greeted Pat with a hearty handshake.

"Pat, it's a fine day for a picnic. We've saved a table for you next to ours. Will you join us?"

"A fine day it is, Matt. Good to see you this morning. We'll be happy to join you just as soon as we get our breakfast."

"We're just by the big oak on the other side of the football field. It's very shady and you'll be able to see the game this afternoon real well," Matt said on his way to the table with a plate of pancakes in his hand.

Breakfast was everyone's favorite at the Casserly household and today was very special. Kate and Pat watched as each child choose from eggs, bacon, ham, fried potatoes, and pancakes. They each filled a plate and headed for the table that Matt Dougherty had saved for them.

"Good morning Kate," said Mary Dougherty. "My your family looks fine today."

"And your family too, Mary. I don't know how you contend with five boys," replied Kate. " I believe you'll go straight to Heaven, Mary."

"Aw, Kate, your startin' to sound like Pat flattering me like that. That'll be enough of that. Let's all eat and enjoy the day," replied Mary. "Maybe we'll finally have a peaceful day. Since it's all Irish here and we don't have to contend with that gang of Modocs."

"Amen to that Mary. I said my rosary three times last night and asked the Blessed Mother for a peaceful day. There's Father Ryan. I'll call him over to give us a blessing. Father Ryan! Father Ryan!" Kate exclaimed.

Father Ryan heard his name and walked over to Kate. "Good morning Mrs. Casserly, Good morning, Mrs. Dougherty. Patrick. Matthew. You all look fine today."

"Good morning, Father," Kate said. "We are all about in our seats now, can I ask you to give us a blessing?"

"Why certainly, Kate. I would be happy to." Father Ryan said as he moved to spot where all could see him and raised his hands out over them. "May God almighty bless you with health, peace and happiness on this day and forever more. In the name of the Father, Son and Holy Ghost, Amen. I must leave now so you folks have a nice day. Matthew, my son, be sure I don't find you involved with those Mollies. You're a good man and the church needs good men. Good day to you all."

Mary just looked at Matthew and lowered her head.
She knew about his involvement with the Mollies. At
first she thought it was a good thing that he was
standing up for those who could not help themselves
but since the long strike, the increased violence, the
Coalies, and now the excommunication, she was no
longer sure. It was too late for Matt. He knew way
too much to be allowed out of the organization, surely
he would be killed.

"Well let's eat!" Pat said loudly to break the silence
of an awkward moment. They all started to eat and
talk. What a great day it was going to be.

Everyone talked and laughed and had a good time
during breakfast. It was one of the few times that
folks could get together and relieve the tensions and
trials of daily life. It was a time to let down your
defenses and just have some fun. The children were
the first up from the table. The girls went one way,
the boys another. The adults stayed to talk and finish
coffee, but soon too they would go their separate
ways. The women usually stayed around the tables,
always ready to take care of the next skinned knee or
elbow. Worse yet, to massage the aching joints of
their husbands as they tried to be young again. The
women would talk about how the coal companies were
so unfair to their husbands and sons. Some would

knit, others darned socks or crocheted lace. None knew what the answer was. There was a faction that sided with the Mollies and clandestine methods. Others thought the new ways of John Siney and his nonviolent strike methods were the answer. The memory of the long strike was too fresh. All they were really sure of was that they didn't want to go through that again. Many of the old women remembered the famine in the old country. They came to America so it would not happen to their children.

Most of the men congregated at the quoit pits. This was a very popular game among the older men, those that finally realized they were no longer able to play football like a school boy. The picnic grounds were home to no less than a dozen quoit pits. Where there were no formal clay pits folks would just improvise. The pits were made of 3 foot square pits of clay with a steel hog in the middle. The hog was about 18 inches long and about 5/8" in diameter. It was driven down into the clay until only 1" protruded. The quoits were iron, flat on the bottom and rounded on the top. The top was called the hill and the bottom the hole. The quoit could be no more than 8 ½ inches in diameter with a hole no more than 5 ½ inches. It typically weighed around five pounds. The game was played with the hogs placed eleven yards apart, play alternating between players, each throwing two quoits.

Each player was allowed an assistant called a "lighter."
It was the lighter's job to stand at the far pit and
decide the strategy for the throwing player by placing a
small piece of white paper at the players aiming point.
A ringer scored two points and if a second ringer went
on top of the first only the top ringer counted. If a
quoit topped the hob it would count as one point and
block any attempt at a ringer unless, of course, you
could flip it off the hog with your quoit. If no ringer
was scored, the closest quoit would receive one point,
toppers beating touchers. Play continued until one
player reached twenty-one.

Pat was an accomplished quoit player and Matt had
become his trusted lighter. Matt knew Pat's throwing
skills so well, there was no strategy that they could not
play. Pat had grown to trust Matt's ability to spot their
opponent's weaknesses and capitalize on them.

The games continued throughout the day, Pat
winning many more than he lost, when just after
supper as evening approached the ultimate challenge
came.

"Casserly!" cried out Frank McHugh. "Folks are
saying that you're playing well today. Care to take me
on?"

McHugh was Schuylkill county champion in the
annual contest held at Pottsville. Last year he bested
Francis O'Boyle from St. Clair in a best of five match,

winning three consecutive games to take the championship. Tommy Dugan was Frank's lighter and most folks said there was none better.

"I'm not sure I'd be any competition for you Frank," Pat replied modestly.

"Come on Pat we can take him," said Matt.

"You're not afraid of me are you Casserly?" Frank always pushed. He wanted his opponent's emotions to play against them.

"Fear has nothing to do with quoits." Pat responded. "After all it's just a game." Pat knew that this would provoke Frank and play on his emotions as well.

"Well Casserly, you'll not best me with mind games today. Let's take it to the pits."

"Agreed Frank. We'll need an unbiased judge. How about Father Ryan?"

Frank knew he could not argue against Father Ryan. "OK, Father Ryan it is. I'll meet you at number three in ten minutes."

Word spread around the grounds like wildfire. Everyone knew Frank McHugh's reputation as a Molly and everyone knew Pat's abhorrence of the Molly's methods. Would Father Ryan call a clean game or would he hedge to Casserly, a good churchman? Most expected that Father Ryan would keep it clean and fair, even though he had no use for McHugh. And then there was Matt, Pat's trusted lighter. Could he be trusteed or would he throw the match to his superior in the A.O.H? The crowd stopped everything they were doing and headed to number three.

"Bernie. Our dads are playing Frank McHugh and Tommy Dugan in quoits. Come on let's go watch," cried Matt Jr. "This ought to be a real fight to the finish."

"OK, I'll be right there," answered Bernie.

The two joined the ranks on there way to number three, part way there Mike O'Brien meet up with them.

"Well Casserly. I hear you had some troubles with Nathan Garrett. I'd like to help you get even. You are interested in getting even aren't you?" O'Brien was setting his trap. He would use the boy to get Pat to join the Mollies.

"You bet I want to get even, but I'll do it my own way and in my own time. I don't need any help from you or your friends." Bernie was angered by O'Brien's suggestion that he might need help.

"You don't think you can fight Garrett alone do you? He's one of Gowen's men. You try anything against him and the Coalies will be all over you. You really do need our help?"

"I don't know what I will do yet but I will think of something. My dad always says that you should use your head first. It is much better than trying to use force."

"Well you'll see in a few minutes how we can work together. Your old man doesn't have a chance against Frank, Tommy and Matt."

"Matt's on my dad's side, he's his best friend. He won't help Frank and Tommy."

"He will if I tell him to." O'Brien slipped away and let the boys go on alone.

"Matt, what did O'Brien mean by that?" Bernie questioned in confusion.

"The Mollies are very powerful Bernie. They can make anything happen. If O'Brien wants McHugh to win. He will find a way to make it happen. You'll see. I don't think our dad's have a chance at winning this match." Young Matt knew his dad was a Molly but he too was sworn to secrecy and could not admit it to Bernie even though O'Brien certainly had inferred it.

"You're wrong Matt. They'll win and my dad will show you how quoits is supposed to be played."

They neared number three as both players were shaking hands in front of Father Ryan.

"Now boys I'll call a clean and fair match. When I make a ruling it will stand, I'll have no arguments. Do you understand?"

"Yes Father," both replied.

"All right then. Pat, you're the challenger and get to call the toss of the quoit to see who throws first.

Will you have hill or hole?"

"I'll have hill, Father," replied Pat.

Father Ryan then tossed a quoit up in the air flipping over and over until it struck the hard ground; flat on the hole side.

"Patrick you'll throw first. Lighters to your positions. I'll caution everyone here that I won't put up with any shenanigans. Now let's have a clean match." Father Ryan had taken charge of the match and set the stage for all that was to come.

The crowd immediately got noisy as each had their favorite and started to cheer. Matt and Tommy took their positions as Pat got ready to make the first throw.

"Tommy you're in for your first defeat in a long time," said Matt as he put his first slip of paper down just inches behind the hob.

"Don't talk too loud Matt. O'Brien wants Casserly to lose this match and he expects you to cooperate," answered Dugan.

Just then, Pat let go his first throw. It headed directly to Matt's mark and stuck down right on the paper, topping the hob with the back end of the quoit. This was considered the ideal opening shot. The only way to counter was to knock Pat's quoit off the hob in preparation for your second shot.

"Looks like someone forgot to tell Pat he was supposed to lose. Why is this match so important to

O'Brien?" asked Matt as Tommy spotted his paper for Frank's first throw.

"You think O'Brien tells me everything? I'm just a supporting member same as you. You know all the real decisions are made at county level. I just do what I'm told, like a good soldier."

Just then Frank's first throw landed just in front of the hob and just enough to edge right under Casserly's causing his quoit to be a topper under Casserly's. We were in for a classic match if both were to continue at this pace.

Pat's next throw came down right on top of the first two quoits in an attempt to dislodge Frank's topper. Instead it clanked off his own and rolled to the side. A double topper at this point was next to impossible so Frank's last quoit fell off to the side and long, in no way jeopardizing his current topper. Frank went up one to nil.

The match went on, back and forth. It was the most brilliant match anyone had ever seen. Frank McHugh was truly a champion and Casserly seemed to be guided by God himself. Never had anyone seen such tremendous play. The match was now tied at nineteen all. If someone could score two on this turn it would all be over. The excitement in the crowd was at a peak. There was side betting that was doubling with each throw. Not a sole there was doing anything but watching this match. Frank McHugh would throw first.

"Well Casserly, I've played with you long enough. I'm taking it home this round," Frank said as he tried to get on Pat's nerves. "I'll top this one out and that'll be the end of you."

Frank took a long look at the mark that Tommy laid down and an instant later his quoit was on it's way. It flew true to the mark going in just past the hog with the back side topping it nicely. It was the same shot that Pat opened with.

"Very nicely done, Frank. I guess you'll not get two points for a ringer yourself," said Pat.

"It's not over yet Pat. Make your throw," replied Frank.

Matt placed his paper marker down and Pat gave it a long stare. Off flew his quoit on a path to knock Frank's topper off. It hit just long and Frank's quoit held on to its top perch.

"Too bad, Casserly, that was a fine try. Just not good enough."

Frank let his next quoit fly and landed it dead on top of his first throw aided by Casserly's quoit which prevented it from glancing off. The crowd went wild. It appeared that McHugh had won the match. He had a double topper. There was no way that Pat could beat that.

"All right, all right, quiet down now," yelled Father Ryan. "Patrick has a final throw."

The crowd quieted down. There did not appear to be anything left for Pat to try. Matt was down the other end and did not know where to place his paper slip. There appeared to be no solution.

"Step back Matt," yelled Pat to his friend. "I'll need no paper for this shot."

Matt stepped back out of the pit. He had no idea what Casserly was going to do. Pat knew there was only one chance. He had seen it done once before, twenty years earlier. He knew it hadn't been done since. Pat got low in a crouch and started swinging his quoit around and around back and forth but not with the hill side up, as was usual. You see, only quoits that land hill side up count. He was throwing the quoit with the hill side down. Everyone thought he was crazy. He continued his windup and let the quoit fly on a very low trajectory. He had put everything he had into the throw. The quoit speeded along just off the ground, upside down until it struck the hob with such force that the two quoits belonging to Frank McHugh flipped up in the air just enough for Pat's quoit to flip back to hill side up and score a ringer. Two points for the ringer, Casserly wins!

The crowd was stunned for just a second. Had they really seen it? Had Pat Casserly just pulled off the greatest shot ever in a quoit match. Yes, they had seen it. They yelled and cheered, for Pat had done the impossible.

"FOUL!" cried Father Ryan. "Your lead foot was not in contact with the hob. Two points go to Frank McHugh and he wins 21 to 19."

The crowd could not believe their ears. Had Father Ryan taken the win away from Casserly? What could have been his motive? Why would he call a foul on the best shot every seen? Something was amiss.

It didn't matter Pat's supporters were enraged. Joe McDonnelly threw the first punch right into Jim McManhon's face. The brawl was on. Women grabbed the children and headed away as fast as could be. The two sides erupted furiously on each other. Nothing like a closely contested match to create a little tension and this was the best match ever.

O'Brien took this chance to pull Bernie Casserly aside into the nearby bushes.

"I told you I can make anything I want happen. I paid the priest one hundred dollars to make sure your dad would lose," Mike O'Brien said, lying through his teeth. "I told you I have the power."

Bernie pulled away and headed home just as fast as he could. He really did know what to think. He needed some time alone.

The fight wound down quickly. There was too

much beer that day to allow for a lot of stamina. Everyone headed home but none would forget the day.

Bernie was having a hard time sleeping that night. He had too many things running around in his head. Too many questions. It was only about 11:00 P.M. and he decided to go for a walk. He was very quiet as he went down the stairs and out the door. Everyone else was fast asleep. Bernie went up Railroad St. to Catawissa and then turned east on Center St. He walked several blocks and ran right into none other than Mike O'Brien coming out of Mike Flanagan's saloon.

"Well, young Casserly. Are you lost?" Mike said to a startled Bernie.

"I'm not lost. How'd you manage to pay off Father Ryan. He doesn't like the Molly Maguires. He excommunicated all of you."

"Don't you worry lad, Father Ryan's on our side. He just has to do some of the things that he is told, just like everyone else. You need to grow up boy and learn the way of the world. We can help you. There is strength in numbers as long as you stick together, no matter what. We can help you get Nathan Garrett. Alone, you don't stand a chance."

"But my dad always said there would never be an

end to violence unless we all refused to take part."

"Just think back lad. The English have been violent to us for over seven hundred years. Even though we had no possible way to defend ourselves. Power is for those who take it lad. We are going to take it. Are you with us?"

"As long as I can get back at Nathan Garrett I'm with you."

"You go home now lad. I'll get you what you need tomorrow."

Chapter Six

Sunday rolled around quickly and the Casserly's went through the Sunday morning routine without much conversation about the brawl that had ended their glorious day at the picnic. At St. Canicus, Father Ryan felt compelled to change his sermon and instead to speak about the barbarism he had observed the day before. He was filled with anger and told his flock that they had soon better change their ways or there was nothing but Hell's fire awaiting them. The women sat and shook their heads in agreement as the men gazed off into a sea of escape. Nothing would change. The women knew it. The men knew it. Father Ryan knew it.

After church, Kate had made a wonderful dinner of sausage and plenty of colcannon with a fresh huckleberry pie for desert. They all filled their stomachs and were ready to enjoy the day. Pat and Kate decided to take the family on a walk and enjoy the day. Bernie, of course, did not want to go. At fourteen, he was a man and did not want to waste time on a walk. He had more important things to do.

"Well good afternoon to you, Mr. Duffy," said Mike O'Brien as he entered the Merchants Hotel. "Are all the boys here yet or am I the first?"

"Good afternoon, Mr. O'Brien. Wasn't it a wonderful picnic yesterday?" Duffy said with a grin. He knew McHugh had almost lost and was fishing for some information from O'Brien. "Pity how Casserly lost that match after such a wonderful shot."

"Yes Mr. Duffy, it was a pity but the rules are the rules." O'Brien would give him no satisfaction. "I'll be in the back with the lads."

O'Brien entered the back room to see James McKenna staring at him. He always seemed to know when to be around.

"Why if it isn't Mr. McKenna. How were things with your dear sister?" asked O'Brien.

"My sister? Oh yes, my sister is just fine now." McKenna stammered after being caught off guard. "It was a fine time in Philadelphia."

"You promised me that Thomas would be dead by now. What excuse have you this time?" howled O'Brien.

"No excuses, O'Brien. I'll take care of Thomas. It's just the timing has to be right. Besides, you know I had to be in Philadelphia. I'll need to wait until the next big payday to send some men. The celebrating will make for a good diversion. You know how all the lads like to have a drink or two when payday hits."

"Well it had better be soon. You made a deal and I expect you to stick to it."

"Don't you worry O'Brien, Billy Bull Thomas is as good as dead. Now tell me, how are things going with that Casserly fellow? You had a plan to get him to help us," said McKenna.

"That's right, and help us he will. Frank over there just beat him in a game of quoits at the Humane picnic yesterday and by chance Father Ryan called a foul on Casserly just as it appeared Casserly had won the match. I have them all thinking that we paid off Ryan and that he is actually sympathetic to the A.O.H. On top of all that, I have Casserly's son in my pocket now. You see, his son was fired at the mine by that Gowen kiss up Garrett and he wants revenge. I set the whole thing up. I'm going to get the boy some black powder and fuse and let him have his revenge on Garrett. He can blow that son of a bitch to kingdom come."

"Are you sure the boy can do it? And how will that bring his dad to us?" asked McKenna.

"I'll teach the boy how to set the charge, and after Garrett is blown to high heaven I'll tell old Pat that the boy did it out of revenge and the only way to protect him now is with us on his side. We can set up the alibis that will keep the boy from the noose. Surely he has seen it enough times before, the alibis have not failed us yet. Casserly will be on our side for saving his boy."

"I got to give it to you Mike, that's a pretty good plan. I don't see any reason in the world that it won't work. Well, I'll be getting back to Shenandoah now. You lads take care. Oh, and have a drink on me. I wish I could stay but I don't want to miss my train. I'll see you in Tamaqua on the 25th for the convention."

McKenna left three dollars on the table for the boys to have a drink and strode out of the room on the way to the train station where he ran into Captain Linden.

"McKenna, you Irish bastard. What are you doing in Mahanoy City?" Linden said loud enough for everyone around to hear. "Get in my office. I want to have a word with you."

Linden grabbed McKenna's arm and twisted it behind his back with his club resting on the back of McKenna's head. He shoved him through the door to his office and slammed the door behind them.

"Sorry for the rough treatment, Jim. What have you to report?" inquired Captain Linden.

"The trip to Tamaqua was very rewarding. It seems that Alec Campbell set up Hugh McGeehan with his own saloon. A reward for offing Yost. There will be a big convention of the Mollies on the 25th in Tamaqua all the county will be there, well over a hundred I suspect. Lastly, you need to warn Nathan

Garrett that young Casserly, a mule driver that he fired, is planning to blow him to hell. O'Brien is backing him and getting the powder for the job. Well, let's have it, the train is coming and I have to go. How about a small cut over the left eye, that should be enough for this lot?"

Captain Linden drew his knife and put a small cut over McKenna's left eye. Just enough to bleed convincingly. He then pushed McKenna out of the office door.

"Get back to Shenandoah you Irish scum and behave yourself or you'll get much more next time," Linden yelled as McKenna stumbled onto the platform.

The rest of the day went without incident. McKenna got back to Shenandoah. Pat and the family enjoyed their walk. Sure it was a fine day.

Evening rolled around much too soon as Mike O'Brien was hunting for Bernie Casserly. He wanted to deliver the powder as he promised. After all, he didn't want to give the lad too much time to think. O'Brien wasn't the only one hunting. Jess Major had seen him skulking around and decided to follow him. O'Brien didn't have to hunt long, Bernie found him.

"Have you got the powder, Mr. O'Brien?" queried young Bernie.

"That I have, lad. Do you have a place to hide it

until you're ready to do the deed?" replied Mike O'Brien.

"I do." said Bernie. "I've a crawl space under the house. Me and my dad will be digging it out so we can have a proper basement. We only work on it when there is no other work. My dad is so busy now he'll not have time to be digging. I can hide it there."

Jess Major listened intently.

"All right lad, here is the charge and the fuse." Mike handed a tightly wrapped cylinder of black powder, large enough to level a room or two. "Now lad, when you are ready you just punch a small hole in the side and push the fuse in. Then light it and run. The fuse will only give you about thirty seconds. Remember, keep it away from anything hot."

Just then the fire bell at the Humane started to ring and cries of fire started to echo up and down the street. Then the bell at the Citizens started too. The cries soon announced the fire was at the back of Frank Wenrich's butcher shop. This time it was Frank's smoke house and his tool shed that were ablaze and he had not used the smoke house in over a month. The Lady Jane Smith from the Citizens was the first to roll followed quickly by the Humane's hand drawn hose cart. They were lucky it was very early evening and not everyone had gone to bed yet. If they got there quickly enough they would be able to contain the blaze.

Mike O'Brien ran to help with the fire. Bernie ran home to hide his powder and fuse. Jess Major followed Bernie.

Bernie arrived at the house in a full trot. He went around back to the hole that had been cut through the stone foundation into the crawl space. It was very dark. Bernie grabbed a candle which was kept just inside and lit it.

"Where should I hide this?" Bernie said to himself.

He found a small, shelf-like area just under one of the floor joists. He set the candle down so he could see and placed the fuse and the charge on the shelf.

"Bernie! Is that you Bernie?" Kate cried out the back door.

Bernie quickly scurried out the hole in the foundation.

"Yes mom, it's me. I just heard about the fire and thought I would stop and tell you I was going to help dad at the fire."

"OK Bernie, be careful. I'm putting the children to bed now so you and your father be quiet when you get home."

"I'll tell him mom," Bernie said as he sped off to the fire.

Kate went back into the house to make sure the children would get a good night's sleep. There was school in the morning and the weekly routine would start early. Michael was the first to bed. He was very excited over hearing the fire bell and wanted to wait for his father to come home. Pat always told him how the fire went and explained how the whole effort had gone. Kate was very insistent and after a little struggle got him in bed. Elizabeth and Catherine were only slightly more reasonable, both wanting to wait up for their father and brother. With a little effort they too went to bed. Kate came back down to the kitchen to wait for her men to come home.

Bernie met up with Pat at the fire at Wenrich's butcher shop. They had all done a good job and limited the fire to the smoke house and the tool shed. Things were starting to wind down when Frank Wenrich came out of the butcher shop with his rifle, a Winchester repeater he had just bought. He fired two shots into the air to get everyone's attention.

"I want to know who did this and I want to know tonight. Mollies or Modocs, it makes no difference to me. I've had my fill of your fighting and bickering, and I mean to put a stop to it. Now, who will speak up so we can put and end to this?" Frank was mad as hell and everyone knew it.

There was a long silence and Frank spoke again. "I knew you were all too yellow to fess up. I can tell you the new vigilance committee will investigate and get to the bottom of this, I'll see to it. The decent citizens of Mahanoy City will restore order. I'll have no more Irish or Welsh stench stinking up this town. Not as long as I have a breath in me."

Again a long silence. This time it was interrupted by a large BOOM, an explosion. It shook the surrounding houses. It was not only heard but felt by all.

"My God! What have you bastards done now?" Frank cried out.

I think it came form back by the railroad tracks just a block or two down. They looked down the street and back toward the tracks. The smoke was just starting to rise and the flames were not far behind.

"Let's get this hose rolled up lads and get on our way," cried Pat. "It looks like it's down by my house. Hurry!"

Bernie put his hands over his face. He couldn't remember. Did he put the candle out? "No. It couldn't be that. It had to be something else." he said to himself.

The Citizens and the Humane both cleaned up quickly and were on their way to the fire in moments.

As Pat rounded the corner leading the men pulling the hose cart; he screamed, "Kate!" He realized it was his house that was now in flames. He dropped away from the cart and ran down the street to get to his

family. Bernie followed closely behind. Matt
Dougherty was already there on the front porch roof
pulling the window from its frame. He was crawling
through the front window when Pat and Bernie
arrived. The back of the house by the kitchen was
fully engulfed in fire. Bernie went through the front
door and headed up the steps. He knew his two sisters
slept in the back of the house. He opened the
bedroom door and the two of them were huddled on
the floor crying.

"Get up now!" he cried as he grabbed Catherine
under the arms. "Elizabeth come help me!"

Elizabeth got up and helped Bernie get Catherine
to the front room. There they met Matt Dougherty as
he was climbing out the front window with Michael in
his arms back onto the porch roof. They were all
coughing badly as Bernie pushed the two girls to the
window. Outside Pat was on the roof and took young
Michael from Matt's arms.

"Where are the girls?" Pat cried to Matt.

"They're coming now," Matt said as they appeared
at the window. "I'll help them get out. You take
Michael."

Just as the girls were coming out of the window, a
ladder hit the porch roof and up came Frank Wenrich
to help.

"Hand the boy to me Pat. I'll take him down,"

said Frank.

Pat handed Michael to Frank and then got on the ladder himself so that he could get the girls down to safety. He got below Catherine and helped her down the ladder. Then Matt Dougherty followed guiding Elizabeth. They were all safe on the ground.

"Where's Bernie?" cried Elizabeth. "He was right behind me at the window."

"He must have gone back in. Where's Kate?" said Pat. "Matt, watch the children I'm going back in."

Pat threw open the front door and was met by a wall of smoke. He hesitated for just a second and went in. As he got to the stairs he stumbled. It was Bernie. He quickly picked him up and headed for the door. He was met by Frank Wenrich at the door who took Bernie from his arms as he crashed to the ground from lack of air.

Frank took Bernie across the street with the rest of the family. He was still breathing but had lost consciousness. Frank held him up and began patting him on the back. Bernie revived and quickly hurled his stomach contents to the side. Pat struggled across the street to join them barely conscious himself.

"Pat, you and the boy took in quite a lot of smoke. You sit here and rest we'll handle the rest," said Matt.

"Matt, where's Kate? Find Kate for me and bring her here," said Pat.

"I'll find her Pat. You just rest," replied Matt with a grave look on his face.

Matt could see that the entire back of the house was in flame. The boys from both fire companies were hard at work trying desperately to save something. The fates were kind that night and they soon had the fire under control. They had managed to save most of the house. Only the kitchen was badly damaged.

They still hadn't found Kate.

Soon they were able to enter the back kitchen area where the fire had started. There was no doubt that the fire started here, everything was badly burned. They searched the kitchen thoroughly but did not find Kate. They went through the archway past the basement door toward the living room and there they found the body of Kate Casserly. It was covered with debris from the fallen ceiling but there was no mistaking it. She had been walking toward the living room when the explosion happened. She never stood a chance. It was a miracle that any of them escaped.

Matt Dougherty walked slowly toward Pat and what was left of his family. The girls were hanging one on each arm and Pat held Michael in his arms. Bernie sat on the side by himself.

"Pat, Kate is dead. We found her body in the living room. She must have been knocked out by the blast," Matt hung his head as he finished.

"No, that can't be. It must be someone else. It can't be Kate," Pat said in denial.

"Dr. Hermany is already back there," said Matt.

Pat jumped up and ran to the back of the house. Matt stayed with the children. Bernie just sat and cried. Saying to himself over and over. "It's all my fault. It's all my fault."

Pat got to the kitchen just as Dr. Hermany was having Kate's body removed on a stretcher covered with a blanket.

"Can I see her Dr. Hermany?" Pat pleaded.

"Certainly," replied the doctor as he pulled back the blanket.

Pat fell over Kate's body in tears as he hugged her lifeless form. "My dearest Kate, how could I let this happen?"

Dr. Hermany put his arm around Pat's shoulder, "Come Pat, come with me now. The boys will take her to the undertakers, Haughney's I suppose. He will take good care of her."

Pat put the blanket back over her and dropped his head down on her and cried. As he raised his head he screamed in anger, "I'll get the rotten bastards who did this. I won't rest until I do. I promise you Kate. I'll get them."

Chapter Seven

The fire left Pat feeling empty. He loved Kate
more than anything and it had taken her and his home.
Frank Wenrich had a house on Mahanoy St. which he
offered to Pat until he made his repairs and got back
on his feet. The wake was held at this house. Of all
the fires that had occurred, this was the first that had
resulted in a death and the whole town was in
mourning.

Pat sat at the table in the kitchen with young
Michael next to him. Bernie sat on a chair in the
corner curled up in a fetal position. The rest of Pat's
friends filled the small kitchen. They were drinking
heavily, drowning their sorrows as it were. There was
plenty of whiskey, tobacco and snuff. Some played
cards while others told stories. It was the third night
and all were weary. The women were in the front
room surrounding the casket where Kate's body lay.
As was the tradition she was laid out in the casket
which sat upon four chairs. She was all in white with
only her hands and face showing. On her chest was a
hand-carved crucifix which Matt Dougherty had
provided. In her hands was her own rosary which she
had worn down over the years. Her two big toes had
been tied to prevent her from returning as a ghost.
Father Ryan had worked hard to obliterate the old

traditions but some things would not go away. The worst tradition was the drinking. Try as he might there was no stopping the men from drinking.

Some of the old professional mourners were there in a back row of chairs. They would ask no fee for this wake, they were truly devastated. Elizabeth and Catherine were with Mary Dougherty, Matt's wife. She sat with them on the couch. All the women were clutching their rosaries, praying and keening over the loss of Kate.

Father Ryan entered the living room accompanied by two alter boys. He asked that all gather to pray for Kate. Mary Dougherty went to the kitchen to ask the men to join them. Pat took Michael by the hand and lead him to the living room. Matt Dougherty followed with a few more friends behind. Bernie stayed in his chair. Matt was going to get him but Pat stopped him.

"Leave the lad be, Matt," said Pat. "He will have to learn to face this on his own. He's a strong boy and will come to accept this as time passes. Right now he just can't believe all this is happening."

Father Ryan lit the incense in his censer which was carried by one boy. The other boy carried the Holy water. He began. "Let us pray. We are here to pray for our departed sister, Kate, who comes to join You, oh Lord. This heinous act has taken her from us all too soon and surely the perpetrators will be severely punished." He took the censer from the alter boy and began his prayers in Latin as he swung the censer over Kate's body. The mourners in the rear began to wail and cry. Next he took the Holy water and blessed Kate's body. The entire room was filled with tears as Father Ryan finished with the service. Tomorrow St. Canicus would be filled as all gathered for the final mass after which they would all walk to the cemetery to send Kate off to her final reward.

"It's time to take her now," said Father Ryan. "Are the pallbearers ready?" Six of Pat's closet friends surrounded the body and closed the lid. They picked the casket up and kicked over the chairs as they proceeded from the house. Father Ryan led the procession to the church. Kate would lay there until morning. She was in God's hands now and safe from the fairies who would steal her soul. All was done properly; they would not get this soul.

St. Canicus Church was full the next morning. Father Ryan was at his best. He did his best to keep it about Kate but, nevertheless, he chided the flock about the continuing violence. He pleaded with them not to seek revenge. This tragedy should be enough to convince anyone that more violence will lead to more tragedy. Most of the congregation sat in tears, nodding their heads in agreement. The Mollies sat straight backed with firm commitment and revenge in their eyes. They knew that they had to answer. They knew that the time had come. They would not let this deed be the end. There would be no justice against the Modocs. Only Mollie justice was the way to deal with those heathens. After all, the Modocs had no regard for an Irish life.

The procession to the cemetery was long and slow. Pat and Kate had many friends and they all turned out to mourn Kate's passing. The cemetery service was short but pointed. Father Ryan again cautioned against revenge. Kate was now truly in the Lord's hands. Father Ryan dismissed the gathering and they began the long walk back down the hill. It was time for the healing to begin.

As they approached Main Street they were watched by Jess Major and Big Bill Jones.

"Look at that bastard, Casserly," Big Bill said with anger in his voice. "I suppose those Irish slime think we're responsible. I'll bet the damn Mollies themselves set that blast. You know how much they want Casserly to join them. What a devious way to get him to join them. Kill off his wife and blame us. I guess we'll have hell to pay now."

"Then hell it will be," replied Jess as he dropped his head and turned away from the procession and marched away from Jones.

Jones caught up quickly. "What are you saying

Jess? All out war?"

"That's up to Casserly. I got my revenge. I don't think he'll bother with me now. He's a spineless, gutless, ugly, Irish toad. Serves him right for screwin' with me."

"What are you saying, Jess? You know something about this?"

"Sure. I saw young Casserly get something from Mike O'Brien so I decided to follow him. O'Brien went to Frank's smokehouse fire. Young Casserly sneaked into the crawl space under the house with it, then came back out to go to the fire. That was my chance. I crawled in to see what O'Brien had given him. It was a black powder charge and a fuse. The bastard was going to attack one of us. I decided I could stop that and get my revenge all at once."

"You rotten bastard. You killed an innocent woman."

"An Irish woman. What's it matter?"

"A woman just the same." Big Bill turned and walked away shaking his head.

"Mind your loyalties now Bill. Remember what you are."

"Oh I'll remember. When the whole world comes down on us, I'll remember. When we're all rotting in hell, I'll remember."

Pat took his family home and gathered them in the living room.

"Elizabeth, I know you are only eleven, but you are now the woman of the house. It will be very hard for us with your mother gone, but gone to the Lord she is. We are left here and we must pull things together and carry on until we go to meet her. Catherine and Michael are old enough now and won't need your full attention so it will be a little easier. You will need to leave school so you can keep up with all the work around here. It will be very different but we will all adapt as long as we pull together. Does anyone have anything to say?"

Bernie put his head down and thought about what he should say. He had done nothing but think about it. He decided that no good would be served by him coming forward with his story. He would have to bear the guilt himself, for the rest of his life. He was responsible for the death of his mother. Yes, it was an accident, but if he hadn't been so fixed on revenge it never would have happened. Father Ryan was right. Now he decided to just put all his efforts into making life better for his sisters and brother. He would make it up to them somehow.

No one had anything to add.

"OK then. Let's get on with it. Elizabeth, time to

start supper. Catherine and Michael you help. Bernie, I want to speak to you."

Elizabeth, Catherine and Michael headed to the kitchen. Bernie and Pat went out on the front porch to talk.

"Well Bernie, you were right. I can't believe I was such a fool. This god damn thing has gone too far. Those Modocs did this to me. That Jess Majors and the rest of his cronies. They'll be no justice either. Mike O'Brien and Matt have been after me to join the A.O.H. They say that it is the same here as it was in Ireland, the English rule and we get nothing. I was willing to try a new way in a new land but they are right. We have no power to do anything as long as there is no justice. Lad, it's time for fighting. We need to stand together for our rights. I will talk to Matt tomorrow and I will ask every man I know if he is willing to help. It must be a calculated plan though. One that will change the way things are going. We need to get the old Germans with us instead of with the English."

"But Father, you always said that revenge and violence were not the way." Bernie said with all the courage he could muster.

"I was wrong son. My way got your mother killed."

Bernie had no more courage for that day. He

dropped his head and went into the house. Pat stayed on the porch and just looked out at the sky, as if he could see Kate.

"Kate, I promise you I will get the men responsible for taking you from me."

Chapter Eight

Pat had his meeting with Matt Dougherty and was quickly inducted into the A.O.H. It couldn't have happened at a more opportune time. You see things were really beginning to heat up in the Mahanoy valley. There was hardly a day went by without another new event. Truly, it appeared that war had begun. Fall gave way to winter and soon the cold February winds were upon them. They never knew how cold it would be, as what was left of the Mahanoy City Chapter of the A.O.H. meet to discuss matters. Matt Dougherty was now the bodymaster. Mike O'Brien and Frank McHugh had both been arrested by the Coalies, charged with conspiracy to murder Thomas, Major and James. Original members present included Dan Dougherty, Joseph Boyle, Jamie McGinty, Pat Sheridan and Frank McDonald. New members present that came over with Pat were Bernie Casserly, Big Mike Dugan, Tom Dugan (Mike's brother), Pat Dillon and John Quinn although Pat had brought twenty-eight additional members with him.

"Well lads, it's time to take stock of ourselves," Matt said as he started the meeting. "There have been too many arrested. We'll need to get some money together to pay the lawyers and we'll have to get our alibi stories straight. O'Brien and McHugh will be back with us in no time. I suspect that we had an informer in our midst. Let's take some time to see what has happened in the last several months. I have some *Miner's Journals* for the last few months. Let's see if we can find a clue to who the informer might be."

"I think everything started back on the August 14 payday," said Pat. "Squire Gwyther of Girardville was shot and Kehoe blew the arrest. Then, here, Bully Bill Thomas and James Dugan got in a gun battle and killed Christian Zimmerman. Then Sheriff Werner let Thomas go. Said it was an act of God. What kind of justice is that?"

"Yes, but that bastard Gomer James finally got his justice," Jamie McGinty interjected. "Hurley did a clean job on that I'd say"

"Then we got Sanger and Unger over at Heaton's colliery," Pat Sheridan said with a big grin. "Two more deserving souls there never were."

"Don't forget Jones down in Lansford. Kelly and Doyle really screwed up getting caught by Parkeman," Matt said with a perplexed look on his face. "Do you think one of them turned squealer?"

"Even if they did," Dan Dougherty said. "How would they know who was doing things here and in Shenandoah?"

"Good point, brother. I think we need to think about someone who is moving around a lot. Let's keep going."

"It ain't bad enough that all the arrests are happening but then the bastards had to strike out at widows and pregnant women," cried Frank McDonald. "That action at Wiggans was an act of the devil himself. I think they thought they were getting Jack Kehoe. They had no need to shoot everyone else. Poor Charles O'Donnell, why there was hardly anything left to bury. It was a stupid move. Kehoe's too smart to get caught like that. They'll never get him."

"Yes and then they arrest Frank Wenrich when the Widow O'Donnell identified him and the sons-of-bitches let him go too," an exasperated Pat Dillon exclaimed. "Why is it justice is only for them and not us?"

"Now calm down Pat," yelled Matt. "We don't want to lose our heads now. It's time for clear thought, before someone else is arrested. We need to remember they just convicted Michael Doyle for the Jones job. We don't want them stretching any necks around here."

"You know I've been thinking," Bernie Casserly stunned them all since he rarely spoke. "That guy from over in Shenandoah, you know, McKenna. He seems to do a lot of moving around. Always passing through here one direction or another. Could he be the informant?"

They all looked at each other, surprise all over their faces. The boy was right. He was the only one around that meet with all the A.O.H. chapters, but he was Kehoe's right-hand man. How could he be the informer? You could see the questions rolling through their minds. He was a stranger, not from around here. He said he came form Buffalo, but who checked?

Matt broke the silence, "If James McKenna is a Pinkerton then we're all dead men."

They stared at the floor in deep thought, each man thinking of what he had done and why he was there.

Pat Casserly broke the silence this time, "You all know I'm new to this group and was not a party to past events. I never supported your actions. I always felt we could work with the English. I WAS WRONG! The path you have chosen at least gives us a voice. Without resistance to their tyranny they would keep us down forever. Maybe some of us will die. I feel it a small price to pay for our freedom and our rights. If we can't get our message out things will never change. We deserve better treatment. We must continue this fight as long as we have breath. We must stand together, united in our cause. I have been passive and cooperative all my life. Where did it get me? The bastards killed my wife and I almost lost my children as well. Just last week they took another one

of us and didn't even wait for a trial. Pat McKeever
was an old friend. We all know it was not an accident.
He was unconscious well before that coal car crushed
him. Pat had been around too long to have had that
kind of accident. He was much too smart to have
been there. I've had enough of this foul treatment.
It's time to take the fight to them."

Big Mike Dugan was the first man on his feet.
"I'm with you, Pat," he said as he started to clap.

The others rose one at a time. "Me too." The
clapping increased until all were standing in support of
Pat's words.

"Let's get back to order now," cried Matt
Dougherty. "We've got work to do. I think we should
all go home now and think about what our next step
will be. For now we will sit quietly and see what cards
our enemy will play next. We will meet here again next
week to discuss our next move."

Each one rose and headed to the door on his way
home to think. Some to plot, some to worry. There
was no doubt the war was at its peak and they were
losing. There had been arrests all over the coal fields,
but there had been arrests before. The leadership was
all in jail. It was big this time. There was already one
conviction. The contrived alibis didn't hold up. Yes,
something was different this time. Surely they knew
that for every testimony given against a Molly there

would be twenty loyal Irish to counter it. How could the jury ignore that?

But something was different this time and his name was Franklin Gowen, former prosecutor for Schuylkill County and now President of the Philadelphia and Reading Railroad. He wanted the Mollies shut down and he had the resources to do it.

Bernie and Pat turned the corner to head to the house and were meet by twenty Coalies with Linden in the back.

"Grab them boys!" Linden yelled.

"Run Bernie," Pat cried out.

It was too late they were caught by surprise. Pat fought like an animal. It took six Coalies to get Pat on the ground, three more were holding Bernie. Face down in the mud Pat asked, "What's this all about? Why are you doing this? I've done nothing you'd be interested in."

"Relax Casserly, it's your boy we want." Linden answered.

"Bernie? The boy's done nothing. Let him go. I am responsible for taking him to the A.O.H. It's me you want, take me."

"Oh, I'm sure we'll be back for you too Casserly. You should have stayed away from that lot. You were a good man. Now you are one of them, a stinking

Hibernian. I have nothing to charge you with, but your boy here . . . well that's different. Bernie Casserly!" Linden exclaimed. "You are charged with the murder of your mother, Kate Casserly. It was you that started the fire that killed her. I'll see you hang boy. Killing your own mother. I'll see you hang."

Pat cried out, "It's not true. It's not true. The boy was with me. Don't talk to them son, we'll get you out real soon. Don't tell them anything to make matters worse. We'll get you out. Don't worry, they won't hold you long."

Bernie couldn't speak if he wanted to. He had lived with his guilt long enough. He knew in his heart that it would all catch up with him sooner or later. He was tired of living the lie. Now the truth would come out and he would hang. He knew this could happen and decided to face up to it if it did. The Coalies dragged him away as Linden stayed behind with his men and Pat. He didn't want any trouble from Pat. He waited until they were well on the way with Bernie in tow.

"Casserly, we're going to let you go now but we don't want you following us. Crack him boys."

One of Linden's men raised his club and brought it down on the back of Pat's head. Pat felt a dark cloud blot out his sight. He went out cold and laid there, face down, in the mud and ice as Linden and his men marched away.

Chapter Nine

November 1876, much had happened since Bernie was arrested in February. The convictions were coming, one after another. Campbell, Doyle, Donahue and Kelly are found guilty in Carbon County for the murders of John Jones and Morgan Powell. In Schuylkill county, Boyle, Carroll, McDuffy, McGeehan and Roarity for killing Tamaqua policeman Benjamin Yost. Thomas Munley for the Uren and Sanger murder. All were sentenced to hang. All thanks to Jimmy Kerrigan who turned states evidence and James McKenna, whose real name was James McParlan, a Pinkerton. Mike O'Brien was convicted as well thanks to Frank McHugh. Frank too had turned on his friends to save his skin. Franklin Gowen returned to the court house in Schuylkill county to take control of the prosecution and he had been very successful. He spent a large sum of money on getting rid of the Mollies and he didn't want anyone to mess it up. He had gotten the leaders and the rest were too scared to cause him trouble. Now Frank Gowen had one more trial, Bernie Casserly. He thought Bernie's crime was the worst yet and he wanted him hanged. He wasn't bothered by the fact that he had only hearsay evidence. It hadn't hurt him so far.

Pat had gone to Pottsville several times each month

to visit Bernie and he watched the boy grow worse each trip. He had withdrawn and hardly spoke. He was torturing himself while he awaited his inevitable death. Pat was unable to reach him. His attorney, Harry Dornan said he could not help him if he wouldn't talk to him. He did promise Pat that he would do what he could, but he thought his chances were very bad. The trial was ready to start and Attorney Dornan had no defense.

"Your honor, you have seen me here many times before," Frank Gowen spoke with authority. He was looking as fine as ever in his custom tailored suit. "We have seen the convictions of many men. Men who committed heinous crimes against honest hard-working citizens. But this man, Bernie Casserly, has done the most heinous crime of all. He killed his mother."

Pat looked over at the jury and saw them nodding in agreement. There were six Germans, who spoke little English, four Englishmen and two Welchmen. It seemed like Bernie had no chance at all.

"This is an easy case, your honor. I need only one witness to make the story clear. I would like to call Pinkerton agent, Mr. James McParlan to the stand."

James McParlan entered the court room through a side door. He was constantly guarded by Pinkerton guards. The Mollies would surely like to see him dead. He took the stand and the bailiff swore him in.

Frank Gowen approached the witness stand and began his questioning. "Mr. McParlan can you please tell the court how the defendant murdered his mother."

"Yes sir, I will. It all started with Mike O'Brien, the Mahanoy City bodymaster. Mike wanted to attract new members to the Ancient Order of Hibernians. He wanted to use Bernie Casserly to entice his father Pat to join up with them. Pat was influential in the Humane Fire Company and would bring many members with him."

"And how does that lead us to Bernie killing his mother?" asked a smug Gowen.

"Well the defendant was fired from his mine job as a mule driver by Nathan Garrett, the superintendant. The defendant wanted to even the score. O'Brien, on the other hand, wanted Pat Casserly. So O'Brien gave the boy some powder to blow Nathan Garrett to kingdom come. It all went sour when the defendant there tried to hide the powder under the house until he was ready to do the job. Well, your Honor, the powder blew up right under the kitchen where his mother was. He almost killed the whole family."

McKenna sat with a satisfied look on his face. This was his last trial and he knew the boy had no chance, not after all the other convictions.

"No more questions," said Frank Gowen with confidence. The ball was rolling and this would go quickly. This was Gowen's last trial as well. He had gotten almost all the leaders, crippling the Mollies, at least that's what he thought. He would leave the clean up to the local district attorney from here on. He had a business to run and had spent enough time on this already. He was the victor and to the victor go the spoils. With the Mollies out of the way, he could now concentrate on profits for his company. There would be no more disturbing strikes, no more wage increases. He was in charge now.

The defense had no questions. Dornan knew it was over. Gowen went through his summation and so did the defense. The jury listened intently to Gowen, they all but ignored Dornan, and then retired to deliberate.

Pat had never seen a trial before so he didn't really know what to expect. What he did know was that his son Bernie would not fare well. This is the first time he heard the story. Bernie hadn't spoken about it at all. There were no direct witnesses, no one to testify against Bernie except James McParlan and his statements were only hearsay. The defense attorney pointed all this out in the summation. There was a reasonable doubt. After all Bernie was at the fire with many others. Seven witnesses testified in his behalf. Surely the jury would believe them. But had they even listened?

It didn't take long, the jury was only out 50 minutes. Hardly enough time to take a vote after all the formalities were over with.

Judge Pershing entered the courtroom, took his seat and called for order. "Mr. Foreman, have you a verdict?"

The foreman stood and addressed the bench. "Your Honor, we find the defendant, Bernie Casserly, guilty as charged."

The court erupted. Pat was red in the face, furious at the verdict. He got up from his seat and headed right for Gowen. Three guards brought him to the floor. Two more bound his hands. They dragged him from the courtroom screaming, "I'll get even with you Frank Gowen. I'll see that you get yours." Pat had now lost his wife and his son to this senseless battle. His heart was filled with revenge.

Bernie just watched in silence. In his mind he knew he was getting what he deserved. He just couldn't face his dad with the truth. What did it matter anyway? He would die now and at least his dad had some hope that it wasn't true. At least he didn't have to face him.

The judge brought the courtroom back to order.

"Bernard Casserly," the judge said. "You have been found guilty of murder. The murder of your own mother. I must admit that I don't understand how it happened but I must enforce the law. For this crime you will be hanged by the neck until dead." His gavel came down and with it, all hope for Bernie Casserly.

Chapter Ten

The trial had been over a week and the Casserly household was very somber. How could they hang a boy only sixteen years old? Was there no compassion? Would no one help? They were doing their best to hold out hope. Father Ryan had been very supportive and visited the Casserly household several times a week.

Elizabeth was thirteen now and try as she might she could not understand. She had become an adult overnight, too fast for anyone. Ever since Kate died she had to take care of the house. She always helped and she always mothered Catherine and Michael but this was different. She had two children depending on her. Gone were the days of worrying about the next spelling test. She, like the boys in the breaker, had lost her childhood too. Elizabeth worked from sun up to sun down. She had even taken in laundry to help out. This was no life for a young girl.

Catherine was ten now and she really missed her mother. She was still in school and doing very well. Elizabeth worked with her every night, drilling into her the importance of her education. It was all right with Catherine. She loved to learn and she loved to read. Each night she would read to Michael before bed while Elizabeth finished the day's chores.

Seven-year-old Michael was another story. You could barely keep him still. He had a hard time in school since his mind was always elsewhere. After school he would run with his friends sometimes forgetting to come in for supper. Elizabeth could not bring herself to yell or spank him. She even found herself covering up for him so dad wouldn't find out. Pat always found out. He too found himself forgiving Michael prematurely. Michael was now his only son, he thought. Even though Bernie was not yet hanged Pat found himself focusing on Michael as if he were. He felt lost and alone, powerless with nowhere to turn. It was the first time in his life he felt truly alone.

The Casserly household had been in turmoil much too long but it wasn't going to be over until June. Judge Pershing had set the execution date for June 21, 1877. There would never be any getting back to normal for the Casserlys. There couldn't be. Pat had vowed to work for justice and he would find a way. Somehow justice would be served.

Elizabeth called everyone together for the noon meal. "Michael, please be quiet." They each took their places and Catherine gave the blessing. As she finished a knock at the back door startled them. Pat got up to see who was there.

Pat opened the door and stared in wonder and then

in anger. It was Big Bill Jones, a Modoc. A man he had tangled with many times before. Pat was ready to slam the door...

"I know you have no liking for me Pat but I need to speak with you." Jones held his hat in his hand and dropped his head, staring at the floor. "May I come in?"

"I've no reason to speak with the likes of you Jones. You're not welcome in this house." Pat had all he could do to control his anger. It was seething inside him.

"You have every reason to kill me where I stand Pat but that won't help your son."

"What's my son got to do with you?" Pat said quite startled by the thought.

"Your son's innocent. I know who set the charge." Jones was still staring at the floor. "Please let me come in. My life's not worth a cent if I'm seen here."

Pat turned to Elizabeth, "Take the children upstairs. I need to talk to this man alone."

Elizabeth gathered Michael and Catherine and quickly took them upstairs, each with a piece of bread and some cheese in their hand.

"Come in Jones. This better be the truth."

"I'd have no reason to tell you this if it weren't." Jones said as he stepped into the kitchen. "Jess Major set the charge, Pat. He'll kill me for sure for telling you but I can't see a sixteen-year-old boy hanged for something he didn't do. I won't testify against Jess but I can't see an innocent boy hanged. I couldn't live with myself. What can we do to get Bernie out?"

Pat sat and thought about what he had just heard. His mind raced with questions. Why now? Was it true? Did it matter if it was true? What could they do about it? Who would believe this story? Pat could only think of one thing, saving Bernie.

"Let's go Mr. Jones. We're going to Pottsville." Pat yelled up the steps to Elizabeth. "Mr. Jones and I need to go to Pottsville. Take care of the children, we'll be back tonight."

Pat and Bill Jones headed out the door and up to the Philadelphia and Reading station. The next train to Pottsville left in ten minutes, with luck they would be in Pottsville by 3:00, just in time to catch the judge. They did not leave unobserved, Jess Majors saw them heading to the station. It didn't take him long to put things together.

"That bastard Jones has told Casserly what happened," Jess said to himself. "I'm a dead man if I hang around here." Jess was on the next train to Philadelphia. He would stay there until he found out what was going to happen. No one would find him there.

The trip went well. The train pulled into the

Pottsville station at ten minutes to three. The two headed immediately to the courthouse to see the judge. As luck would have it the President Judge Cyrus L. Pershing was coming down the hall heading to his quarters when Pat cried out.

"Your Honor, we've got a new witness. You're hanging an innocent man."

The judge turned quickly to see Pat with Big Bill Jones trotting right behind. "Your Casserly aren't you?"

"Yes your Honor, I am. This man here is Bill Jones, a Modoc, and he has something to tell you."

"All right, follow me to my quarters."

The two men walked closely behind the judge and soon were standing in front of his huge cherry desk. The judge took off his robes and sat behind his desk. "Now then, what is this new evidence?"

Bill Jones stared at the floor and then began. "Your Honor, I'm truly ashamed of myself for letting this get this far but I feared for my life. It's true what was said in the court room, Bernie Casserly did get a powder charge from O'Brien but it was not Bernie that set it off. It was Jess Majors."

"How do you know this?" asked the judge as he fixated on Jones.

"Jess told me himself sir. He told me he saw O'Brien give the charge to young Casserly and that the boy hid it under the house. Then the boy went to the fire and Jess went under the house. Jess knew Casserly was planning something. He thought he could stop that and get his revenge. He hated Pat Casserly because Casserly was a better man then he was. He had hated all the Irish since they killed his brother George. Ever since then he didn't care what happened to anyone who was Irish. Casserly was not like the others and this riled Jess even more. He saw his chance and he took it and a fine woman was killed in the process."

"Revenge?" questioned the judge.

"Yes sir. He wanted to avenge his brothers death."

"You are an honorable man Jones. It takes great courage for you to step forward now. I believe you."

The judge got up from his chair and went to the chamber's door. "Mrs. Schmidt, get me a deputy please right away."

"Right away your Honor." said Mrs. Schmidt his secretary of ten years.

It took less than a minute and the deputy was in the office. The judge was just putting down his pen as he walked in. "Deputy take this note up to the prison. These two men will be going with you. Release the boy, Bernie Casserly, he's innocent and I won't have an innocent man spend any more time in jail."

Pat could hardly believe what he heard. "Your

Honor, you are truly a good man. Thank you. Thank you."

"No thanks are necessary Casserly. Justice is not about hanging innocent boys. My heart was never in this sentence to start with. I'm glad Mr. Jones came forward, it was a brave act. It's bad enough you lost your wife, you shouldn't lose your son too. Take him home and rebuild your family."

"Thank you your Honor. God will look kindly on you." Tears streamed from Pat's eyes. He finally had something to rejoice about. He had seen justice. He would take his son home.

Bernie, Pat and Bill Jones were on the five o'clock train headed for Mahanoy City. Bernie was trying to understand what Bill Jones was saying.

"You mean I didn't cause the explosion?" finally words came from Bernie's mouth. A spark of life also came through.

"That's right lad. Jess Major set that charge after you left." Big Bill Jones had all he could do to hold back. He had done something to help someone. It really didn't matter that he was Irish. It was very wrong what Jess did and it was very wrong to let the boy hang for it.

Bernie hugged Pat, tears flowing down his cheeks. "Can you ever forgive me father? If I had only listened to you I never would have had the powder and none of this would have happened. I just wanted to get even with Garrett."

"You're just a boy in a man's world. A very complicated world. It's hard to sort things out sometimes and even harder to forgive someone who has harmed you. I am just as much to blame. I should have found a way to support the rights of our people. This is America. A place where justice is for everyone. Everyone with power that is. Well it's time we had power too. Not through violence but by educating our children, by voting for our own representatives, supporting each other, and placing people in the government is the way for us to take our place in this society."

Pat threw the door open and yelled in, "We're home! Look who's here with me."

Three children ran into the kitchen to see their father and their brother Bernie. It was a happy reunion as they all hugged. The Casserly family could now start to heal.

No charges were ever filed against Jess Majors since Bill Jones refused to testify. Jess eventually returned to Tuscarora. Pat lost the first election at the Humane but would go on to win the election in December 1877. He continued with the A.O.H. as well but it was different now. They concentrated on electing councilmen and county officials. Mahanoy City had changed too. There was still friction but slowly things improved. The coal mines were all consolidated under big business. The small operators became fewer. The labor movement continued its struggles. The road ahead was long but they were here to stay and continue the fight for Molly's justice.

Bernard Casserly Family

L to R: Sarah (Sally) Dreisbach, Bernard
Casserly, Bernard Jr., Anna, Patrick.
Bernard and Sally had one more son, John.

Timeline

The timeline is based on the one created to keep the book in historical order. The book is a work of fiction and some liberties were taken. The most prominent being the moving of the excommunication.

May 26, 1875

James (McParlan) McKenna visits John Kehoe and discovers that Mahanoy City is in a bad state. There was an attempt to kill Dan Dougherty in the beginning of May. Kehoe wants an all out street war. Dan Dougherty was acquitted of killing George Major in Lebanon when the bullet from his skull was removed and it was shown not to be from George Major's gun. The real killer was John McCann who fled back to Ireland.

June 1, 1875

The Mollies meet in Mahanoy City to hear Dan Dougherty's case against William M. (Bully Bill) Thomas and William and Jess Major. The Major's were working in Tuscarora. County Tresurer Chris Donnelly and John Donahue of Tuscarora would take care of the Major brothers. Mike O'Brien, James Roarity and John Kehoe would take care of killing Bully Bill Thomas.

June 4, 1875

James (McParlan) McKenna, Thomas Hurley, Michael Doyle and John Gibbons journey to Mahanoy City to attempt to kill Bully Bill Thomas. McParlan decides to postpone the job since there is a big union march from Shenandoah to Mahanoy City and the state militia is there to keep order.

June 27, 1875

McParlan learns that Bully Bill Thomas is to be attacked the next day.

June 28, 1875

Morris, Gibbons and Hurley attack Bully Bill Thomas but are not successful.

July 5, 1875

Benjamin Yost is murdered in Tamaqua. This is a pivotal event. One that, arguably, leads to the formation of vigilance committees.

July 15, 1875

James McParlan goes to Tamaqua to investigate the Yost murder. Bully Bill Thomas is attacked again and is shot at while going home to Shoemakers on a Lehigh Valley train. He jumps from the train as the shots narrowly miss him.

July 17, 1875

James McParlan returns to Shenandoah where he sends a report to Pinkerton boss Franklin outlining a plot to kill John P. Jones, mine superintendent.

July 25, 1875

James McParlan goes back to Tamaqua to see Jimmy Kerrigan and meets Mary Ann Higgins, Kerrigan's sister-in-law. McParlan spent $2.65 on drinks Alec Campbell sets up McGehan in a tavern business as a reward for killing Yost in a clean job. The tavern opens 8/14/1875.

August 14, 1875

Pay day at the mines in Girardville, Shenandoah and Mahanoy City. the Miner's Journal of August 20 reported on what they termed a spree of drunkeness.

William Love shot Squire Gwyther of Girardville. Constable John Kehoe arrests William's brother Thomas allowing William to flee.

A drunken Bully Bill Thomas gets into a street shot out with James Dugan in Mahanoy City. Many shots are fired by both men, one lodging in Thomas' cheek. One shot went wild and killed German miner Christian Zimmerman who was waiting for his wife outside a store while she shopped. Another man was shot in the leg and another stabbed. Thomas was arrested for the attack on Dugan but no charges were ever filed for the killing of Zimmerman, it was written off as an act of God.

Gomer James, acquitted of the murder of Irishman Edward Cosgrove in 1873, was shot and killed at the picnic of the Rescue Hook and Ladder Company of Shenandoah. The picnic was held at Glover's Grove and James was tending bar. Thomas Hurley did the shooting. Hurley had also been involved in the first Bully Bill Thomas shooting.

August 25, 1875

The Mollie convention was held in Tamaqua with over 100 attending. One member was expelled for tipping off Jess and William Major to the attempt on their life in Tuscarora.

Captain Linden warns McParlan that the Welsh and English are planning their revenge on him.

August 31, 1875

McParlan wakes up and finds Mike Doyle sleeping next to him. Doyle has a Smith and Wesson pistol which he borrowed from Ed Monaghan. Doyle tells McParlan that he was going to Raven Run to shot mine boss Sanger. James Friday and Charles O'Donnell and James McAllister from Wiggans would assist with the job.

Body master Frank McAndres calls a meeting to shot mine boss Reese. He needed a deal with Kerrigan to do the job so he sent John McGrail, Mike Darcy and Thomas Munley to Summit Hill to kill Jones. He sent McKenna along to make things right with Kerrigan.

September 1, 1875

Hurley and McParlan were in Muff Lawler's Tavern at 8:30 in the morning when Doyle, the O'Donnells, McAllister and Thomas Munley came in after the murder of Sanger and Unger at Heaton's colliery.

September 2, 1875

Shenandoah Herald editor Thomas Foster comes out strongly in support of vigilance committees.

September 3, 1875

John P. Jones shot at Lansford by Edward Kelly and Michael Doyle (not the same Doyle that stayed with McParlan) both of Mt. Laffee. The job was arranged by Kerrigan. They were arrested by a Tamaqua Posse led by William Parkeman.

Captain Linden returns to Shenandoah to find out that one of his officers tried to question a suspicious man and was fired upon. The officer returned fire and killed the suspect.

September 4, 1875

The Tamaqua Courier comes out in favor of Vigilance Committees.

September 6, 1875

Father McAvoy, founder of St. Canicus church in Mahanoy City, dies at St. Theresa's in Philadelphia at the age of 46.

September 20, 1875

McParlan goes to New York and completes the list of all known Mollies in Luzerne, Northumberland, Columbia, Carbon and Schuylkill Counties. The listing showed residence, occupation, standing in the society and crimes committed. The list was then published in the major newspapers, 347 AOH names were listed. A mysterious handbill was also circulated marked "Strickly Confidential." It outlined all the acts from Bully Bill Thomas to John Jones and listed all the participants and towns. It appeared to be a Pinkerton publication but no proof was ever given.

September 29, 1875

McParlan contributes $2.00 to the Kerrigan, Kelly and Doyle defense fund. They hire James B. Reilly and Len Bartholomew as defense attorney's.

October 4, 1875

McParlan goes to Wilkes-Barre to avoid the Vigilantes and pretends to raise money for the defense fund.

October 9, 1875

Payday Saturday results in incidents all over the region.

In Shenandoah, an English miner was shot. In a different tavern a Welsh-man, John James, had his throat cut and was robbed of $500 and his watch. Both survived but no arrests were made.

October 19, 1875

McParlan goes to Mauch Chunk to the trial. The defense witnesses were readied but the trial was postponed until the January, 1876 term.

October 29, 1875

McParlan is back in Shenandoah making tavern rounds with McAndrew. Muff Lawler tells them that all the Mollies were known and the next time someone was killed they would make it hot for the Mollies. He also said that there was a screw loose somewhere, implying an informer.

Thomas Hurley is arrested for the attack on Billy Bill Thomas and the throat slashing of John James.

The early days of November were marked by uneasiness in the ranks of the Mollies and increased activity by the Coal and Iron police. The were searching and arresting many, including the local constables.

There was also speculation on the origin of the handbill that had been circulated. Was it Pinkerton or was it from the "Vigilance Committee of the Anthracite Coal Region"?

McParlan raises bail for Thomas Hurley, who promptly flees.

Molly distrust runs high and many are expelled in internal AOH trials.

November 2, 1875

General John F. Hartranft incumbant Republican governer was re-elected. It was reported that the Mollies had secretly sold their vote in anticipation of favors.

November 30, 1875

Archbishop Wood's papers contained a copy of a memo written by him from Benjamin Franklin to Franklin Gowen. It lists all the murders from 10/20/1874 to 10/30/1875 and is dated 11/30/1875

December 8, 1875

McParlan reports that Mollies from Gilberton and Wiggans beat rival clan Irishman Quinn from Gilberton near St. Nicholas.

December 10, 1875

Friday 3:00 A.M. - Massacre at Wiggans Patch

Present were the widow Margaret O'Donnell mother of James Friday O'Donnell, Charles O'Donnell, Ellen O'Donnell pregnant wife of Charles McAllister, their infant child and four paying guests; Tom Murphy, John Purcell, James Blair and James McAllister (Charles' brother).

Ellen McAllister is shot dead.

James McAllister is shot in the arm but escapes.

James Friday O'Donnell escapes.

Charles O'Donnell is dragged outside and shot 15 times in the head. His clothes were set on fire burning him from hips to chin. He was then shot 10 more times in the torso.

Others were let go. It would seem that they wanted the O'Donnell's since a note was found at the house the next morning that said, "You are the murderers of Uren and Sanger."

That morning Dr. Phaon Hermany, the Mahanoy City coroner, arrived at the scene. He examined the bodies and empaneled a jury at the scene and began questioning Mrs. O'Donnell. He asked her if she recognized any of the men in the attack. Then John Kehoe arrived and interupted, ordering her not to answer. He said this would be handled another way. Kehoe's wife was Mrs. O'Donnell's daughter, making him a brother-in-law to both Ellen McAllister and Charles O'Donnell.

Later in the day after the coroner's hearing Mrs. O'Donnell identified Frank Wenrich, a highly respected butcher, councilman and former Chief Burgess of Mahanoy City, with assaulting her with a gun but Kehoe pressed the charge and Wenrich was arrested and sent to Pottsville the next day for his protection form a highly excited crowd.

The Tamaqua Courier and the Shenandoah Herald were appalled by the action of what they had heretofore encouraged.

December 11, 1875

McParlan reports that the Mollies want vengeance. McParlan was so distressed over the killing of a pregnant women that he tenders his resignation at 8:00 A.M. The same day. Kehoe states that he is sure Frank Wenrich was involved but will wait and handle it when things calm down.

Shenandoah Herald editor Foster is condemned.

December 12, 1875

The case against Frank Wenrich falls apart when Mrs. O'Donnell states that John Kehoe told her to identify him. Wenrich returns to Mahanoy City where he is greeted by over 300 cheering supporters wishing to shake his hand.

Much speculation followed regarding the perpetrators of the Wiggans attack. Some though it a rival clan action since Quinn was beaten, there had been other fighting between the Gilberton and Wiggans families. However, the incident was well organized, all with masks and oilcloth coats. Some even thought Kehoe did it because Charles O'Donnell was becoming a security risk.

December 15, 1875

Archbishop Wood issues his excommunication of the secret societies intended for the Mollies. The Mahanoy Plane priest was Daniel O'Conner, Father Ryan in Mahanoy City and Father Reilly in Shenandoah.

February 1, 1876

Doyle is convicted of the Jones murder and is sentenced to hang on 2/23/1876. Jimmy Kerrigan turned informer on 1/28/1876.

February 4, 1876

Carroll, Duffy, Roarity, McGeehan, Boyle and Campbell are arrested and taken to Pottsville based on Kerrigan's testimony. The Mollies are stunned.

February 10, 1876

Thomas Munley arrested in Gilberton. Charles McAllister wrongly arrested in Wiggans.

February 16, 1876

James McParlan learns from Mary Ann Higgans (Kerrigan's sister-in-law) that he is suspected of being an informant.

February 23, 1876

The habeas corpus hearing for Munley and McAllister.

Frank McAndrew tells McParlan that they are taking bets that he will testify as a detective. Kehoe warns others to beware of McParlan.

McParlan goes to Girardville to see Kehoe to ask for a trial. Kehoe sets the trial dates for March 1st or 2nd in Ferguson's Hall, Shenandoah.

March 7, 1876

McParlan leaves the coal fields only to return as a detective to testify at the trials.

April 13, 1876

Edward Kelly sentenced to hang for the murder of Jones.

May 6, 1876

McParlan announced as a witness in the first Yost trial. He testifies for four days.

May 14, 1876

Franklin Gowen sends a letter to Archbishop Wood stating that he will vindicate Father O'Conner. O'Conner was accused of telling Kehoe that McParlan was a Pinkerton.

Suggested Reading

Bimba, Anthony, *The Molly Maguires,* International Publishers Co., Inc., 1950, ISBN 0-7178-0273-6

Broehl, Jr., Wayne G., *The Molly Maguires,* Harvard University Press, 1964, Library of Congress Card Catalog Number 64-21239

Conway, W. Fred, *Those Magnificent Old Steam Fire Engines,* Fire Buff House Publishers, 1997, ISBN 0-925165-19-0

Dublin, Thomas, *When the Mines Closed,* Cornell University Press, 1998 ISBN 0-8014-3462-9

Hoobler, Dorothy and Thomas, *The Irish American Family Album,* Oxford University Press, 1995, ISBN 0-19-512418-9

Kenny, Kevin, *Making Sense of the Molly Maguires,* Oxford University Press, 1998   ISBN 0-19-511631-3

McKeever, Eric, *Tales of the Mine Country,* Eric McKeever, 1995 ISBN 0-9643905-0-7

Oley, Norm, *Germanville,* Valhalla Books Inc., 1996, ISBN 0-9657050-0-5

Perez, N.A., *Breaker,* Houghton Mifflin Company, 1988, ISBN 0-395-45537-5

Petrillo, F. Charles, *Anthracite and Slackwater: The North Branch Canal 1828-1901,* Center for Canal History and Technology, 1986, ISBN 0-930973-04-6

Percival, Gwendoline E. and Kulesa, Chester J., *Illustrating an Anthracite Era, The Photgraphic Legacy of John Horgan, Jr.,* Commonwealth of Pennsylvania, Pennsylvania Historical and Museum Commision and Anthracite Heritage Museum and Iron Furnaces Associates, 1995 ISBN 0-89271-065-9

Pinkerton, Allan, *The Molly Maguires & the Dectectives,* Dover Publications Inc., 1973ISBN 0-486-22898-3

Rinker, Harry L., *The Schuylkill Navigation: A Photographic History,* Canal Captain's Press, 1991, ISBN 0-9613675-2-0

Steve Varonka

Molly Justice is Steve's first fiction book. Inspired by his trek into the genealogy world in a search for his roots. Steve proposed a "what if" and the book began to evolve. Prior experience in producing family genealogy books helped drive the decision to try some fiction. Further inspiration was provided through his research readings of *Tales of the Mine Country* by Eric McKeever and *Germanville* by Norm Oley. Real motivation came after reading *Making Sense of the Molly Maguires* by Kevin Kenny. The support of Professor George Turner of Bloomsburg University of Pennsylvania was a valuable asset. Lastly, there is Flash McDonald and Tommy Symons of the Orange and Green show, who, each week, re-minded him of his Irish roots.

Steve is currently a Facilities Manager for the Geisinger Health System in charge of the Wilkes-Barre area. Geisinger Wyoming Valley Medical Center is his base of operations. He joined Geisinger in 1983 after managing a mobile home sales lot and a seven year association with Beneficial Finance. Steve holds a B.S.B.A. in General Management from Thomas A. Edison State College, Trenton, NJ granted in 1997 after nine years of independent study. He is a 1970 graduate of Mahanoy Area High School.

Mr. Varonka says about his book, "I decided to write the book because of the influence of my grandfather Pat Casserly. Since my father died when I was just a baby my only male influence was my grandfather, who lived just next door. Although he was only half Irish you would never have known that by looking at him. In his mind, he was Irish. I also wanted to provide a vehicle for people to better understand the turmoil of the region and time without getting too bogged down in a pure history. The Molly era is indeed a controversial one. One marked by corporate greed, class distinction, ethnic prejudice and injustice. My hope is the book will be more widely read and will prompt some to investigate further."